JONAH

A Gay Teenager's Journey For Love Through the Magical Realism of Faith

JAMES E REESE

Jonah: A Gay Teenager's Journey for Love Through the Magical Realism of Faith

By James E Reese

Copyright © 2021 by James E Reese

All rights reserved.

Library of Congress Cataloging-in-Publication Data is available upon request.

ISBN 979-8-9850234-0-4

Ebook ISBN 979-8-9850234-1-1

No part of this book may be reproduced in any form or by any electronic or mechanical means, including information storage and retrieval systems, without written permission from the author, except for the use of brief quotations in a book review.

Names, characters, and places are products of the author's imagination. Any references to real people, or real places or historical events are used fictitiously.

Book Cover Design by ebooklaunch.com

This work is dedicated to the queer teen in the mirror whose greatest love is his own.

James E Reese

1

Sinner's Lake

Jonah stood in his underwear on the newly painted black box, holding his hands down in front to cover himself, thinking if sin had an odor, it would smell like fresh paint. And the harder he tried to scrub away the pungent, oily black pigment that was his sin, the faster it spread over his body. But it was the paint fumes, mixing with the fusty lake breeze and sweetness of spring that had him wanting to throw up. Maybe if he did, they'd take it as a sign, call their work done and go home. He knew better and couldn't stop picking at his shame or resist scratching itchy belt welts across his lower back.

Searching for a distraction from the stinging guilt and nausea, Jonah eyed over his shoulder the procession of summoned believers shuffling out of the woods, cutting a trail down the grassy embankment and across the flat sand until they found a safe place to his right. A few benignant parishioners wore their street clothes. Reserved families had their men in black and ladies cinched in simple dresses and head scarves. But the pious proudly showed their faith—clothed in traditional white-hooded tunics. Churchgoers who passed him quietly, probably didn't know, but those scowling members obviously did. He expected dirty looks from the other teenagers, not their parents. Even out here, the faithful gathered into their usual cliques: families' together, singles keeping respectable distance from the opposite sex, and chatting widows, who hand fanned their powdered faces and delighted in hearsay in the midday heaviness. Choir members, dressed for the event in their satin gold performance robes, came next and filled in the space to his left.

Mortified by the assembling crowd, there wasn't much he could do, being a scrawny fourteen-year-old sinner, awaiting his spiritual intervention. Maybe he should give them an incredible performance. Test their faith by flailing his arms and shouting nonsense. Contort his body and give everyone in town something to talk about besides politics and weather. Something inside held him back. His adolescent frame suddenly felt hollow, tied together with string, like a thumb puppet toy ready to collapse.

Out of the crowd, Jonah spotted his parents standing in a prayer circle with the two deacons who were responsible for taking his clothes. Their heads were bowed and he could only guess what they were thinking. They had barely spoken to him on the drive out here.

As modest waves splashed against the shore, Jonah gauged his distance to the trees, confident he could reach the woods before they'd catch him. Even barefoot. He'd gotten good at running. Had lots of practice running from bullies, running away and running from himself. Bolting down the track, he even tried outrunning his past, outrunning his mistakes, but ribbons and trophies couldn't make up for his innocent crime or win back his parents' love now that he was suspended from heaven.

Jonah looked down at his sandy feet. "No running today…" he whispered. Reality had them tied; knowing he'd been ghosted at school and had no real friends. With nobody to trust or places to hide, running seemed pointless. He needed to face his demons.

The canvas of dirty waves rolling across Sinner's Lake made Jonah think the wild rumor was true—that the once clear water darkened over the years from the sins of the newly baptized bornagain. The hypocrisy was obvious. This was where the wicked came to find their way and where youth came to lose theirs. Why weren't those gawking teens standing next to him and being judged too? Maybe their parents didn't care like his.

On the bordering cliff's heaven-spot, 'Jesus Saves' was spray-painted with white blockbuster letters. Jonah turned his attention towards the flat grey sky, "Are you really watching? Do you even exist?" He put God to task but a bird's persistent cawing interrupted his efforts.

The sinister black bird—perched in a long-standing tree that loomed in the distant sky—cawed like a barking dog. "Maybe it's waiting to peck out my eyes?" he speculated and then couldn't get the gruesome idea out of his head. "This is the last place I'd hang out if I had wings," Jonah told himself as the choir began their low chant. When the cawing abruptly stopped, he quickly checked the tree again, and saw the bird was gone. Any solace he felt in the bird's disappearance waned away as Reverend Learne approached.

Jonah tried to get a quick look as the big man cut right in front, but was shrouded by the black clothes that wore him—his large bolero hat blocking Jonah's prying eyes. The preacher walked a straight line into the lake and Jonah's heart dropped into his stomach. "Skinny kid," he tried to prepare himself, "remember to close your eyes and hold your breath. God willing, you'll get through this somehow." At least broken faith was better than none at all.

His own breathing suddenly drowned out life around him. His lips trembled over chewing his hurt like fresh gum that left the bitter taste of his parents' betrayal. He even resented the water at the moment because he couldn't swim well. Mostly, he hated himself, because he knew Jesus wasn't watching. Jesus doesn't save queers.

. . .

Standing waist-deep, twenty feet from shore, Reverend Learne asked the Lord for wisdom and guidance while his assembly waited. Carrying the fate of the world on his knotted shoulders, the bearded man straightened his spine, suspended his hat onto his back, then unfurrowed his brow and welcomed his flock with outstretched arms.

> "At the feet of the Lord," he proclaimed, raising his arms to heaven.
> "At the feet of the Lord," parishioners repeated.
> "We weep for mercy," Learne beseeched.
> "We weep for mercy," they reiterated.
> "Open my eyes that I may see."
> "Open my eyes that I may see."

The Reverend made the sign of the cross and took another minute to collect his thoughts as deep creases returned to his face. "Sinner's Lake…" he gestured at the water, "lies at the feet of the Lord." His voice commanded attention. "We come here to confess our sins and seek atonement. We come here to find purification and admission into the Lord's kingdom. We come here today for Jonah Laidley." He paused to let his words solicit their faith. A hardness came to his face. "Be it known! Evil is among us…driving the country down the fast road to hell. Sin is very popular today. Acceptable even among the faithful. Adulterers, alcoholics, gluttons, murders and rebellious youth," the Reverend counted on his left fingers. Then tallied on his right, "Working on the Sabbath, idol worship, psychics, kidnappers and homo…sexuals." The word hung in his throat. "There was a time not that long ago, when these sins were punishable by death. Not any longer," he vented his resentment. "Not today. *Today*, we pass laws and let lawyers and the courts decide…stealing power from the church."

He broke from his sermon to reach inside his pocket for his handkerchief and pressed sweat off his brow. Held the dampened cloth in his hand and continued his homily. "*Today*, we covet possessions and money over faith, banking our lives on credit. No wait! Now there's cryptocurrency. I think that's what they're calling it. The name should be a warning…" he scowled, shaking his head. "Temptations of easy access make sweeter the fruit… fooling us into filling our lives with excess and our hearts with desires while our souls starve. We are wrongly selfish and proud." The Reverend repeatedly pointed at his chest.

"*Today*, our precious children communicate with symbols, texts, t-shirts and guns. This is our fault, we let this happen." He scratched at his beard, "*Today*…" His tone shifted acrimonious, "If your marriage has soured, you can divorce quicker than the resurrection. You can cohabitate or search for a mate with your phone… like shopping for a house or car." He gripped an invisible steering wheel to make his point. "We let this happen! And we're not done… Because *today*, we've blurred gender lines, added new terms for relationships, and redefined marriage."

He anxiously wiped his brow and waded closer to his congregation. "And like marriage," he castigated, "*today,* if you don't like this church, you have about four thousand alternatives." The thought of it made his blood boil. "Do not become Sunday simpletons!" He blasted his followers with a chastising finger while trying to squeeze the white out of the cloth. "Open your eyes that you may see…" He quickly waved his hand and his handkerchief vanished. There was a collective gasp. "Do not be fooled!" He threw his arms at them and his voice quivered with fury, "Today we must lean on our collective faith to find the sinners among us and pull them from Satan's car!" The Reverend slapped the water into a splash and the congregation erupted with applause and shouts of "Amen!" and "Praise the Lord!"

The choir led worshipers in a hymn, and at the start of the fourth verse, the Reverend motioned for Jonah, who swallowed hard, stepped off the box, and hurried across the sand into the lake. Wading through the chilly water felt like wading through his past. So many unspoken rules. How was any kid to know right from wrong? Had he known his parent's love was conditional, he never would have begged them for a birthday party, or shared his wish to come true. That something so innocent carried so much poison. Turned his life upside down and extinguished their love—leaving him in deep water—wanting to go back in time and wish for something else.

—

2

Ninth Birthday

Jonah yawns and hands his mother another piece of tape which she uses to fix the remaining twisted streamer in place above the dining table. He yawns again. Anticipation over his ninth birthday kept waking him up during the night. Each time, from his warm bed, Jonah checked his desk clock, with his superhero binoculars. The thrill of getting to stay up an extra hour, is now gone and he thinks about his wish again.

"Hey, birthday boy?" Mary calls as she pinches the filled balloon between her fingers and places the rubber ring between her tight red lips to slowly let the air pass into her lungs. She holds her breath and pats the cushion and as Jonah sits next to her, she sings, "You've grown another year older, now know that life isn't always fair. Yes, in just a short time you've made it to nine, but you're still only halfway there!" Her voice sounds like a high-pitched cartoon character. They burst out laughing.

"Can I try?" Jonah begs her.

"Yes, but only once. Helium can make you dizzy." Opening the tank valve, she fills the balloon again, and hands it to Jonah. "Take your time and breathe in slowly." Her voice still sounds hilariously distorted.

But Jonah sucks in all the air at once and grins. "What did the whisker say to the razor?" His amplified voice sounds even higher than his mother's.

Mary shakes her head.

"Chin expecting you…" cracks Jonah, rubbing his chin. He can't stop giggling. "And what did the razor say back?"

Mary doesn't know.

"My friends call me dull. But my name's Nick…"

Mary's love beams. She cups his young face, framed with her same brown hair reaching over his ears, then tickles his ribs. "How did you get so funny and smart?" But she stops when the doorbell rings.

"I'll get it!" Jonah jumps up and runs for the front door.

A small group of kids from church all wish him a happy birthday. He doesn't know them well and smiles. Appreciates his mother even more, as she walks up behind him, and welcomes everyone inside. Some of the kids brought gifts, but none of them match the large, wrapped, rectangular box in the corner of the living room.

"Kids, you can set your gifts on the coffee table," says Mary as she greets the other mothers. "Jonah, please take your friends into the dining room for cake."

He can't wait, the moment is almost here. He's been counting down the days for months, marking them off on his calendar, and begging his parents to let him have a party. The one thing he wants, above all the gifts, are witnesses. The more the better.

The other kids take turns swatting balloons back and forth. He takes his place at the end of the dining room table wearing his shiny birthday hat. Feels strange sitting in his father's chair for the first time which gives him a feeling of power and protection and fatherly love that somehow makes up for his father's absence. Jonah can't remember his father's excuse but lets it go when his mother pushes through the kitchen door with his favorite cake. He can already taste the German chocolate when she sets it down in front of him. As everyone sings Happy Birthday, Jonah counts nine candles then counts them again to be sure. Everything has to be right.

"Make a wish, Jonah," Mary beams with pride.

He sits up straight, head-flips his hair to the side and inhales. Then closes his eyes, concentrates on his wish and blows, while the other kids cheer and clap and watch. When all his air is gone, he quickly opens his eyes, sees trails of smoke. What's that? One candle still flickers. It can't be! Now his wish won't come true. His mother leans over quickly, gives a short puff, and the flame is out.

"Happy Birthday, Jonah."

But his mother's delicious cake can't make up for his disappointment. Nor can he wait a whole year to wish again—it will be too late. "Mama??"

"We'll talk about it later," she whispers when his father wheels a shiny new bike through the kitchen door.

"Happy Birthday, son!" he declares.

Jonah puts on his favorite PJ bottoms and, heartbroken, climbs into bed as his parents come into his room. His father brings with him a strange light that he sets on his bedside table. His mother tucks him under the covers while his father struggles to reach the outlet behind the twin bed.

His mother sits down beside him, "No shirt? You're gonna get cold."

"All done..." says his father, sounding winded.

"Daddy doesn't wear a shirt to bed," explains Jonah in an elevated voice.

"Don't grow up too fast son," says his father. "Life might disappoint you. . ." He quickly moves on, "You really scored big this year, didn't you?"

Jonah exchanges special hand slaps with his father.

"Tomorrow, after church, we've got an aquarium to set up and I promised to teach you how to ride your new mountain bike. It's big but you'll grow into it." He pats Jonah's shoulder.

Consolation prizes thinks Jonah.

"Get some sleep tiger!" he urges.

Jonah sees his mother stiffen when his father kisses her head and flips off the overhead light on his way out.

The darkness can't hide his mother's need to wipe her eyes.

"I have one more gift for you, Jonah," her soft voice is uneasy. "But you have to close your eyes first."

With his eyes tightly closed, Jonah hears a click then a low hum and waits with anticipation.

"You can look now…"

He opens his eyes, slowly at first then wider, his mouth drops to his chest. It's the coolest thing he's ever seen. His room is instantly blue with countless holographic stars drifting all around him and his mother. Purple nebulous clouds stretch beyond the ceiling. His room is practically floating in heaven.

"They're all your hopes and dreams," whispers his mother. She looks him in the face. "So don't worry about your wish not coming true."

"How did you know?"

"Mother's intuition…" She pushes his hair out of his face, "Someone needs a haircut." She holds his cheek and looks closely at him, "What did you wish for, Jonah?"

"I can't tell you or it will never come true."

"Sure it will, I have faith. We made it together, remember?"

Jonah believes her. Knows his mother will never lie to him. "There's a kid in my class named Eden…"

"Do you like Eden?"

Jonah gives a quick nod. "Every day I tell myself to go say hi but always chicken out. I'm afraid of the other boys…"

"Never you mind about them boys, they're just jealous. Now, lay back down, pick out the brightest star you can find and make another wish." She tucks the covers under his chin. "It's that simple…"

There are so many, it's hard to choose, but Jonah catches sight of an approaching star and when it moves over his bed, whispers, "I wish for Eden to like me. I want to be his boyfriend…" Silence follows. Jonah looks up at his mother in their make-believe, artificial heaven, watches her comforting eyes narrow, smile flatted, her expression turn into petrified disgust.

—

3

Initiation

The lake was up to his waist when Jonah decided to look over his shoulder, hoping his parents had come to their senses, had changed their minds, and were on their way to save him. To take him home—to love him again. He quickly knew otherwise, when he spotted his folks with their locked hands; joyfully singing in faith along with the congregation. He turned and kept wading.

When Jonah reached the Reverend, shivering and scared, the water was at his chest. Up-close, the preacher looked even more intimidating in his black cassock and large silver cross chained around his neck. Reverend Learne stared stone faced with pockmarks peering through his tawny beard.

Jonah averted his eyes towards the water and discovered that ripples, miraculously, left no watermark on the preacher's vestment. Jonah broke down, sobbing into his own bent arm.

"I'm sorry. C-c-can you s-s-save me?"

Reverend Learne moved quickly and seized Jonah by the back of his neck like a venomous snake.

Jonah felt his feet come off the bottom.

"What is your sin, son?"

"I'm gay…"

"God cannot hear you!" Learne jerked Jonah by the arm, "Let me be clear about this. Your feet are hanging over fire. You need to get righteous, boy, if you don't want to burn."

Jonah scrambled to find words, "I-I'm a sinner. Unworthy of your love. I beg for mercy and redemption."

"Say it like you mean it!"

"I'm a sinner, Lord. Unworthy of your love. Please forgive me. I don't want to be gay. I don't want to be queer. *I don't want to be a faggot!*" Jonah threw himself against the preacher, sobbing.

Reverend Learne stood Jonah upright, dipped his finger in the lake and made the sign of the cross on Jonah's forehead. "In the name of the Father, I rebuke evil and call out this demon! Angels of judgment, spear his homosexual spirit and cast it into the eternal flame!"

Afraid to look, Jonah kept his eyes shut and waited for the fiend to leave his infested body. When the demon didn't materialize, Jonah tried to retch, but couldn't. The preacher rolled his eyes into the back of his head and began to yell in the garbled dialect of tongues.

Jonah heard a collective gasp and looked over his shoulder to see parishioners fall onto their knees.

Reverend Learne grabbed him by the throat. "Deliver young Jonah from the Devil. Baptize his soul and bring him into your merciful kingdom." Faith and expectation rattled his voice. "In Jesus' name we pray!"

Jonah couldn't breathe and tried yelling but no sound came out, and as he fought to break free, the preacher shoved him backwards. Chanting erupted and time hit the brake. Seconds ticked in his ears as he plunged into the water and through the violent splashing, the Reverend's eyes darkened into black hemispheres, then his arms extended themselves as the preacher pushed him towards hell.

Seconds later, Learne jerked him from the water. Jonah came up coughing and struggled to stand. Stunned to still be alive.

"Open your eyes that you may see. You've been saved!" The Reverend loudly proclaimed another victory. "Baptized in Jesus' name."

Applause erupted onshore.

Wiping wet hair out of his eyes, Jonah looked around expecting to find his world transformed, but as he stood in the lake with his bare feet stuck in the mud, his old adamant life slapped him in the face, turning his let down into tears because he still felt queer. Suddenly, a yellow darter buzzed in front of him—the insect hovered—its large compound eyes shifting and aware. The darter repeatedly dipped its long tail into the water, creating water rings. The skimmer was taken to its own reflection. When Jonah tried to get a closer look, the dragonfly flicked lake water in his face and flew away.

Wiping his cheek, the droplets that clung to his fingertips, caught the overcast clouds, and raised an unexpected idea. Jonah leaned over and found his own shimmering face against the corrugated sky. Rings of doubt rippled his understanding. He stared at his likeness—wanting answers. "Open my eyes that I may see…" The words fell off his tongue. Maybe there's a mirror of truth some faithful can't see or refuse to believe. His eyes widened with discovery. Maybe this was his initiation into divinity.

God's door suddenly opened and light saturated the moment with unconditional love and widening perspective. Jonah could hardly hold onto his excitement as his eyes met the Reverend's. "Who knew, God loves queers…" smiled Jonah as he turned his back and swam for shore.

He met his parents in the swash, who celebrated his return with open arms, and gave praise to the Almighty for their son's redemption.

"Now you understand," his mother crowed, covering Jonah with his robe. "Your father and I made the right decision, telling

Reverend Learne about your secret. We knew he could help." She fussed and combed his wet curls with her fingers. "And now… we get to be a family again." She gave him a quick hug.

"Your mother's right," said his father, placing a firm hand on his son's shoulder. "All that praying, Bible study and church going, convinced the Lord. He knows you're penitent and straightened you out."

Jonah faked a smile.

—

4

Secrets

Jonah laid in his bed sniffling past midnight; watching stars travel up the walls and across the ceiling. He'd always been able to outrun the falling dominoes behind him. Had somehow managed to dodge and jump and placate to reach sixteen, but the glowing stars drifting about the room gave him no comfort, and his eighteenth birthday felt another lifetime to be lived. He could no longer contain his resentment towards his parents and the world and needed someone to blame.

Jonah got up on his knees and confronted the carved figure hanging above his headboard. Where was God's compassion and generosity earlier—when Jonah had needed him most? Passing stars cast a dull glow that made the risen Christ appear small and inanimate.

"Are you mad at me for lying?" Jonah asked in a low voice. But there was no indication of understanding on the Lord's wooden face. "Why won't you help me? I've tried to be good and always made the sign of the cross when I thought I should and whenever I messed it up, I always repeated it at least five more times. . ." His hurt boiled over as he searched for answers in figure's robed, outstretched arms, and in the red stigmata on his feet and palms.

Not finding any, Jonah leaned closer, face to face, his eyes probing deeper. "You look like you're keeping a secret. My mother has one…" Jonah couldn't hold his opinion anymore. "Maybe you're not real. Maybe you're just a mass-produced, religious representation of a god, who can't live up to your fame or our expectations. Time to quit asking…" Jonah wiped his eyes and turned off his celestial star light.

He tiptoed across the dark room in his plaid pajama bottoms and carefully lifted the belt off the hook that his father had intentionally put up earlier as a warning. The heavy black leather slipped through Jonah's palm as he pulled it around his waist, pushed the metal prong into the smallest punch hole, and buckled it, turning its punishment into power. He placed a pillow on his chair then forced himself to sit in front of his computer. Listening for movement outside his closed door as his PC hummed to life. Hearing only silence, he needed to process everything that had happened earlier. Confront the ugly truth—expose it—write about it in his journal.

—

5

Acceptance

Jonah squeezes the tender zit until its creamy guts splatter onto the bathroom mirror. "Ew!" he sighs, relieved the blemish is dead. He wipes off the evidence with a tissue then presses a freshly folded side against his bloody pore until it drains dry. Up close, the hole is the size of a crater. His is fifth zit in two weeks. Why so many? He needs to tell his mother the new cleanser isn't working.

Jonah flushes the soiled tissue, wipes his hands on the damp towel, and hits the bathroom light on his way out. Heading down the hall, he passes his parent's room and finds his mother kneeling beside her bed. She often prays throughout the day. Jonah knows to wait his turn. This time she tucks something between her mattress and the sheet and smooths out the bedspread, then crosses herself a couple times. Before she stands and discovers her audience, Jonah turns around, goes to his room, and listens behind his door. After her footsteps pass by, he waits for the coast to clear, then leaves.

He peers inside his parent's room with his toes in the doorway, checks the hallway again, breaks the unspoken kid rule and enters without permission. Gets onto his knees beside the bed and looks over the scene. Everything has to be put back exactly as it is. His heart is pounding. He reaches under the mattress. What can it be? Feels something—pulls out a multi-folded piece of paper with shiny text. Slowly unfolds it, memorizing how to fold it back, naively intrigued. When the last crease is undone so is Jonah. He's hit with adrenaline and the same wild interest he gets from stealing glimpses of men change clothes in the community pool locker room. Unlike those men, the 'Man of the Year' smiles right at him—confident, tanned and naked; posing in the sun with his muscled arms locked behind his head. He begs for Jonah's attention and tempts his innocence with his broad chest, flat stomach, fuzzy innie, and sheathed dick sheltered in hair.

Jonah has never observed a naked man this close before. His foreskin, primordial and protecting, heightens the man's masculinity, makes him more of a man—solid and intact. He lures Jonah with mystery and desire, and a feeling of belonging to an unspoken fraternity, ready to untie his adolescent yearning. Something else catches his eye—a dragonfly inked under tanned skin on the man's bicep.

Jonah lifts up the mattress and discovers several more folded pictures hidden underneath. His father calls his name and in a panic, Jonah drops the mattress. He quickly folds the man of the year and slides him into his back pocket, arranges the bedding as he found it, and rushes back to his room.

"Didn't you hear me calling?" His father opens Jonah's bedroom door, frustrated.

Jonah is busy listening to his headphones music and roughing out a dragonfly in his sketchbook.

His father stands against his desk and pulls off his headphones, "I need your help cleaning the garage."

His mother also enters with a basket of clothes, "Clean clothes for clean souls…"

Jonah gets up and proceeds to put them away.

"What's that sticking out of your pocket?" his mother asks.

"Artwork…"

"You're getting pretty good," his father says, as he flips through Jonah's sketchbook. "Let's see the one in your pocket."

Jonah tucks the paper deeper, wishing it to disappear, wanting to disappear himself. "Still a work in progress," he backpedals. Tries to blow it off. "Really, it's nothing..." But when he sees his mother's insisting hand, knows he's in serious trouble, riding downhill backwards.

"Come on, Jonah," his father's frustration returns.

Jonah's hand quivers as he hands over the folded image.

"Oh my God!!" His mother's eyes widen, she cups her mouth, and quickly hands off the picture to her husband with disgust.

"Jonah, where did you get that filth?"

He had no good answers.

Red faced, his father demands Jonah answer the question.

Jonah looks at his mother, his eyes plead for her help, but when she shoots him a smug, self-righteous scowl, he knows he'll have to lie. "I found it in a dumpster on my way home from school."

Jonah watches his father reach for his belt. Knows lies can never replace the truth and always bring hurt with them.

"I need you to drop your pants, son."

Peeled back and unprotected, tears flood his eyes, as he begs mercy to the figure on the wall. Implores His intervention. When his prayers go unheard, when clemency is granted, Jonah pitches his resentment back. Bits down hard on his lip, grabs for his comforter, and holds his breath. Then climbs into the Man of the Year's arms as fire strikes his backside.

—

6

Magic Spells & Potions

Jonah shifted in his chair against the pain and continued typing. He could no longer ignore his own heart or chase the dragonfly away—because not being able to hold another guy's hand or kiss him or openly love him—felt like running against a hurricane. Time for him to stop and turn around.

Jonah's heart thumped in time with the blinking cursor. His fingers could barely keep up as he poured out his feelings and didn't look back.

Hear my voice, I cry O'Lord,
Like Adam and Eve,
You trick us into believing in happily ever-after
Ring your vaulted door…
Marketing your dream with faith sold to the masses
Another Sunday passes; lectionary classes
My prayers come down in ashes
You're not answering…

Magic spells and potions can't fix what isn't broken
Communion for the chosen

Love can't be saved
Sermons of acrimony chiding
I'm so tired of fighting—so tired of hiding
The truth inside my faith…

Happily ever-after veering towards disaster
I can't seem to make your dream come true
Fell asleep in Eden. Woke up in hell again!
I guess heaven isn't meant for queers in pews…

Time to forget your happy ending
No more pretending, no more surrendering
Bite the apple to the core!
Swallow hard, take the snake up
Go forth with face up. Can't wait to wake-up
On the outside—naked and alive
Hold the boy in my eyes
Leaving this notice on your door…

It took Jonah less than an hour to cover all of his points. He imagined tacking them to God's door and then walking away. He powered off his PC, put his father's belt back on its hook, and climbed into bed.

—

7

The Choir Director

Jonah sat in the uncomfortable red leather chair and looked around the corner office, filled with crowded shelves, neatly stacked music books, piles of sheet music on the floor, religious keepsakes and stale air. Framed degrees, certificates and inspirational posters covered the old plaster walls. A low, thickly painted window offered indirect light, a view of a sidewalk tree, and an occasional chattering bird.

Behind him, music stands stood like minions, ready to pounce, but it was the grand mahogany desk that intimidated him more, and left little room to breathe. His eyes landed on the placard that read, 'Byron Burns, Choir Director' then shifted focus to the man watching him from behind the desk. Jonah was confused. Wondered how this dapper man, polished in a plaid vest and purple bow tie, could help him. Maybe he'd come to the wrong office.

"Do you know why we sing in church?" Mr. Burns asked as he straightened his tie and briefly gazed out the window behind him.

Jonah shrugged off the question and looked away in an effort to stall and run down the clock that had him in the chair for the hour.

Mr. Burns looked across his desk, "Young man, I'm going to tell you what I tell my choir." His voice was calm but firm. "First, you look me in the eyes, so we can find some trust. Then we rise…"

Jonah forced himself to obey the director's command.

"We don't sing because we have answers. We sing because we have a song. That's my scene. Songs are proclamations."

"Your sign says Choir Director… I'm here for counseling"

Mr. Burns reciprocated with his own shrug then reached across his desk and turned his placard around. The other side read, 'Youth Counselor'. He leaned back in his chair to give Jonah some space. "So what's your song?"

"What makes you qualified to ask?" Jonah's interrogation came out harsher than he intended.

Mr. Burns cleared his throat and pointed to his framed degree. "Let me break it down… *Trustees and Faculty of the LeLand Stanford UNIV, grant the rights, privilege and authority to: Byron Wayne Burns…*" His finger tapped at his chest, *"Who has satisfactorily studied and pursued, and passed all required examinations, on this day has accrued, a Bachelor of Arts in Communication."* He sat up tall, slapped his desk with pride, gave a big smile, and then wiggled his finger between them. "We good now?"

Jonah nodded.

"Then let's get back to communicating. How about you start singing."

"Can't sing," said Jonah.

Burns shook his head. "You keep missing my ride. Do you even like music?"

"Sometimes, when I'm supposed to be doing homework, I follow teen blogs, and watch news videos from around the world. They make my life seem unimportant. Music videos and band concerts are cool. Mostly, I write poetry and keep a journal."

"Anything else you're watching online? Other stuff that you shouldn't be…"

Jonah shook his head.

"You had to have been sent to me for some reason, son."

Jonah hadn't heard anyone call him son in forever. "I'm just tired, Mr. Burns."

"My kids tell me that when they ain't up for talking. Either you stayed up too late last night or you're fidgeting over something that you're scared to talk about. So let me strike a major chord. Your parents tell me you're confused. That you've been struggling with who you are for a while."

Jonah sank in the chair, counted ten steps to the closed door and thought about walking out. His eyes studied Mr. Burn's body language; his relaxed patience and the genuine concern on his face. "My parents are worried…that I'm jerking off in the bathroom every night. Sometimes they listen outside the door."

"Are you?"

Jonah wasn't prepared to answer. The conversation now seemed inappropriate in a house of worship and left him bouncing his leg. He swallowed, "Maybe… Sometimes… I'm not blind yet," Jonah half joked.

"Well, there's much debate on that subject." Burns tapped his pen. "Some would say even kissing is a sin. What you've got to ask yourself, is whether choking the bishop is helping or hurting your spiritual journey. Personally, I think the Lord has more important matters on his mind."

Mr. Burns retrieved a brochure from his drawer and read aloud, "Reparative therapy is proven treatment. Guaranteed to change an individual's sexual orientation, feelings and attractions towards individuals of the same gender. Call for more information and pricing." He made an ugly face and dropped the brochure into the wastebasket. "I'd handle this differently, if you were my son."

"Really?"

"You've got to figure out what you like and you work it out with God."

Mr. Burns made it all sound so easy but Jonah knew otherwise. "Can I ask you a question?"

"Let's hear it?"

"If your son was disobedient or rebellious, would you kill him like the Bible says?"

"Wish I could sometimes but what are you getting at?"

"Why is it fair for people to cherry pick their faith and condemn others for doing the same?"

Mr. Burns' response was quick. "I feel you. I'm not making excuses but you know folks don't read the instructional manual, especially the Bible. They want to be told what to think, what to believe. It keeps folks loyal to their institutions, to their traditions, to the Gospel. They empower themselves by judging others. But all that judging, leaves little room for love, if you ask me. . ."

Jonah tried to wrap his head around what Mr. Burns had said then looked him in the eyes. "I already know... I'm gay." It was the first time he'd said it out loud. The weight of his secret suddenly came off his shoulders.

Mr. Burns looked back at him. "Had a feeling you might be. Anyone else know?"

Jonah pointed up.

"Best to keep it between us three for now. Are you feeling at all suicidal?"

"No..."

"You call me anytime you need help, feel like talking, are you hearing me?"

"Yes, sir."

"Can't have a good kid a like you checking out on me and leaving a great big hole in this world. Far, far too many holes nowadays." Mr. Burns took a minute for himself. "But I do think you've got a lot to process, son. Let me see if I can find some affirming resources to help you sort it all out. I'm sure we can find some online support. Which reminds me..."

Jonah waited as Mr. Burns sorted through his papers, until he found what he was looking for, then handed him a number.

"Deacon Porter mentioned his niece. Haven't met her myself.

Said she helped start a youth ministries group at her church. He said for you to give her a call." Mr. Burns paused, "Jonah, you just need time to find your shine."

"Thanks, Mr. Burns."

—

8

WTS

With his lunch tray in hand, Jonah nervously looked around the noisy cafeteria for an empty stool along the wall. The cafeteria was never full except on rainy days. With all those safer seats taken, Jonah was forced to sit at a table and claimed a lucky seat at the end of one. He set down his tray, held his breath, and eased into the chair. The girl on the other side ignored him as she pushed up her glasses and kept reading her book. But the boy next to her shot Jonah an annoyed look. His friend sitting beside Jonah shrugged and the boys carried on talking.

Jonah rushed to eat his lunch, and from the corner of his eye, stole a glimpse of the girl's picture when the boy across the table, held up his phone.

"Told ya bro. Check her out…"

"Fuck! No way, Clay. Did she post how she did it? How she got up there?"

"Don't be a pube, Keith. Even girls aren't that stupid."

"Well, how do we know the pic's real, huh? Maybe she faked it."

"It's real, genius… The entire Central High student body would ghost her."

"Well, if a backwoods bitch can walk the scoreboard, it can't be that hard."

"Oh yeah? Clearly, math ain't your thing. There's a reason why only five kids have done it. That leaves two hundred and ninety-five losers at this school."

"I could do it."

"Dude, you can't do it alone," Clay scoffed over a mouthful of food. "You gotta have a squad, friends that have your back." He snickered at Keith, "Hell, you'll be up there jerking yourself when the authorities show up and I'll be laughin' from the woods. Ain't worth gettin' expelled or ending up like her…" Clay pointed to the girl in the wheelchair at the far end of their table.

"Oh, bro…" Keith burst out, "I bet she's pissed that she wasn't the first girl to do it."

Jonah looked up from his food, as the girl across from him closed her book hard, got up and left in a huff. The boys ignored her and kept on talking.

"WTS has got to be better than losing your virginity," speculated Clay. "You become a legend. GOAT!"

"And get all the pussy a guy could want!" Keith reached across and popped Clay's arm.

"You're such a fag. . ."

"Hey, I'd suck a dick if they paid me a million bucks."

"Fuck that," laughed Clay. "You're so hard up for cash, you'd suck a dick for fifty."

"Okay, I'd suck it for a hundred but only swallow for like a million."

"Queer app boys will go down…do both for free."

"How do you know that bro?" implicated Keith. "Huh??"

Pissed, Clay reached across and popped Keith back, "Fuck you!"

"Ow Bro, I'm only joking!"

Jonah couldn't help but snicker and shook his head.

Clay turned his anger toward Jonah, "You got something to say, try hard?"

"WTF!" snapped Keith, defending his friend. "Who said you could even sit here?"

"I did…"

A blond girl approached at the table stroking her ponytail against her shoulder. Her wholesome face carried a brightness that reminded Jonah of the stained glass angel in the church vestibule who every Sunday welcomed the faithful with windowed light.

Clay gave Keith a head nod egging him to ask her.

But Keith shook his head no.

Clay nodded again then kicked his friend under the table.

"Hey…" Keith could barely make eye contact and stammered his words. "Is that…your pic? Did you really…walk the scoreboard?"

Jonah couldn't believe Keith found the courage to ask her.

She pulled down on her halter top then leaned onto the table. Even Jonah couldn't help but notice her cleavage. "I'm sure smart fellas, like yourselves…" she toyed with them, looking each in the face. "Can figure that out."

Jonah didn't quite understand the power she had over boys, but was relieved when they quickly got up to leave.

"She's not the same girl, I tell ya!" insisted Keith as they walked away.

"Just shut the fuck up!" replied Clay.

The room got quieter as she sat down.

"Thanks…" said Jonah. His mind raced for clues, "Do we know each other?"

"You're Jonah, right?" She didn't give him time to answer. "I'm Jael… My uncle is Deacon Porter. When you didn't call, he said to find you at school. It took me awhile. You're a quiet fish. . ."

Jonah shifted in his chair. "What did your uncle say?"

"That you have a lot going on. You know parents talk. Think you might be g—"

He cut her off, afraid she'd spill his beans and others might hear. "Don't know yet," he lied.

"Jesus knows, he gave me a friend when I needed one. Now I help other teens the same." She put out her hand, "Give me your phone…"

Jonah hesitated at first then passed it over.

She held it up, told him to smile and snapped a selfie of them together then keyed in her number. "Let's chat later. A group of friends from my church are getting together tomorrow." She handed him back his phone. "They're dying to meet you." Her name was abruptly announced over the intercom with instructions to report to administration.

"Good thing daddy just got elected DA," she grinned.

Jonah leaned forward and quietly asked, "Did you really walk the scoreboard, Jael?"

She flashed a satisfied grin as she slid out of her chair. "I did. Girls can do anything when boys get out of our way. Hey, keep it to yourself, okay?"

Jonah nodded. "You worried?"

"Nope! I'm on team Jesus," she winked. "DM you later…"

—

9

Spilled Salt

Jonah couldn't stop grinning over running his new best time and pedaled home faster. The other runners' intimidations only fueled his determination to beat them. But qualifying in the 400 meter and earning a spot on the varsity roster had only been wishful thinking until today. Even the track coach was surprised by his victory and Jonah relished the stun on his face, as he reluctantly recorded Jonah's winning time into the record book.

Making it home, Jonah rode fast into the back yard, peeled off his mountain bike, and landed it against the house. Rushed inside with his good news.

Blazing through the dining room, he stopped to look at the reproduction of Leonardo da Vinci's Last Supper framed on the wall. Jonah's eyes canvassed the orthodox fresco of betrayal; contemplated the apostles' competing outrage, their gestures of speculation, and disbelief painted on their faces. He shifted his gaze to Judas and then down to the spilled salt beside his arm, left on the table. "I'm not discarded today…" he told himself and then went on his way.

"Mom? Dad? I made the team!" Jonah hurried into the immaculate living room but his parents were not sitting in their usual places. Jesus, who was framed in a grand wall mural above the sofa, looked at him with empathy. The Good Shepherd stood in a sunlit field, holding a lamb and his staff, with his flock grazing along the grassy slope.

The scene, the Lord's expression, always brought Jonah back to the unanswered question—why was he gay? Which still went unheard and unanswered and felt like he was playing cards with himself.

Tired of bringing it up again, Jonah tried a joke instead. "Hey Jesus, why do drag queens go to church?" Asked him softly so his parents wouldn't hear. Waited a few seconds before delivering the punch. "Buffets, beauty tips and *Bingo!*" smirked Jonah. "Read that joke online." When the Lord's expression didn't change, Jonah turned his attention to the large aquarium bubbling in the corner, dropped on his knee and searched among the planted foliage for the two occupants. "There you are," he grinned, as the pair of over-sized angelfish approached the glass.

Mottled in black, white and gold, the fish wielded their long caudal filaments like weapons, with their fins fluttering in the shimmering water.

Jonah admired these magnificent fish that he had raised as young fry and whispered through the glass, "Guess what I did?" One of the angels quickly darted off. "Hey, I'm talking to you guys."

"Jonah?" His mother shouted from upstairs. "Will you please come up to your room? Right now?"

The remaining fish pecked at the glass. "Gabriel, I made the track team. Are you proud of me?" The angel swam closer and looked him in the eye. "Hey, I've got to go. Please tell Michael for me. . ." Jonah winked at his fish and jumped to his feet. "On my way, Mom!" he announced, hightailing it towards the stairs.

Jonah hesitated before opening the door—his gut told him something was wrong—was shocked by the mess inside. His closet had been emptied, drawers were pulled open and all of his clothes were in piles on the floor. His computer was gone and his desk cleared. The wastebasket overflowed with school books and papers. His awards and memorabilia were scattered like trash. The only thing left on the wall was the Christ figurine above his stripped bed.

Jonah stood in his room, sickened. Then bent down and picked up the metal figure lying beneath his shoe. The gold-plated runner, held in mid-step, had broken off the black pedestal, and lost his '1st Place 200 m Christian Runner's Camp' title.

"Deacon Porter called this morning," his mother intoned from the doorway. "We asked him to follow up with Mr. Burns, as a favor."

His parents entered, side by side.

"What did Mr. Burns say?"

"Not much, but Deacon Porter expressed his concern that you might turn to drugs, or Internet garbage, instead of prayer."

"He suggested we search your room," his father interjected.

"Drugs we could deal with," moaned his mother. "But this? How could you, Jonah?"

"How could I what?"

She shoved the piece of paper at him.

He recognized his notice to God immediately. "It was something I wrote a while ago. Forgot to delete it. That's all. . ."

"We've spoken with Reverend Learne again about conversion therapy. He said there are successful treatment centers in the state."

Terrified, Jonah quickly came up with excuses, "I can't go. I have school and track. I'm seventeen!"

"And living in our house," said his father. "This doesn't get to be your decision, son."

Jonah's phone rang. He recognized the church bell ringtone.

His parents eyed each other. "Hand it over!" his mother insisted.

33

Jonah pulled his phone from his back pocket and handed it to her.

"Who's Jael?" asked his father.

"Deacon Porter's niece."

"Have we met her?"

"No, Mom. Her family attends God's Church across town. I met her at school the other day and we've talked on the phone a few times. She's super nice…wants to introduce me to her Bible Study friends this afternoon."

His parents looked at each other and eventually agreed.

"But only after you clean up your room," his mother dictated as she and Jonah's father headed for the door. "When you get home young man, your father and I are going to watch you burn this trash in the fireplace." She wadded up his poem.

Jonah grabbed his phone off the bed and sent Jael a text then rushed to get his room in order. Her reply came back fast "B@sinnnerslakeN2h".

—

10

Trust

Nearing the end of the woods on his bike, Jonah's excitement turned into knots when he spotted the lake through the trees. Brakes pulled his mountain bike to a quick stop and his heavy tires skidded in the sand. He took a minute to catch his breath, used the back of his hand to block out the sun, and scanned the shoreline for others. Not seeing anyone eased his knots. He was happy to be out of the house, away from his spying parents and their orthodox expectations.

Jonah walked his bike into the angling sun and headed across the hot sand toward a distant tree. The monstrous Eucalyptus seemed out of place—alone on a sandy berm above the empty beach. The massive colorful trunk, weathered and scarred, defied gravity with leaning resolve.

Jonah dropped his bike and checked his phone for messages. There weren't any. 'm@oldtree,' he texted Jael; confident she would have no trouble finding him. 'SYS,' she messaged back. He shoved his phone into his pocket, eager to tell her about track tryouts. Still psyched over beating his best in timed runs, being the fastest in the 400 and pissing off those varsity boys. He also wanted to thank her for texting him when she did. He'd kept her secret about walking the scoreboard, not that he had anyone to tell, and entrusted her to keep his secret. If things went well between them, he might even tell her about his crush.

Jonah gulped water against the tree but its thin awning of leaves provided modest shade from the hot afternoon. Bored, he thumbed through drawings in his sketchbook but stopped when he came to the dragonfly. His finger traced over the image. Grabbing a felt-tip pen from his pack, he meticulously drew a small dragonfly on the inside of his forearm and when it was finished, made it permanent with his breath, and certified his work as, "Too cool for rules, school and pools."

Stretched out with his head on his pack, Jonah watched the waves travel between his sneakers and thought again about the pool and his crush. He'd kept the details of that day in a safe place, beyond reach of his prying parents, and mean kids at school. Only the Almighty knew the real story. Jonah had spelled it all out— with harsh words tacked to his door.

Jonah closed his eyes and listened for those lost sounds of laughter and when they reached his ears, he pinched his nose and dove underwater; held his breath for as long as he could.

—

11

Pool

Swimming underwater, dodging bikinis and boardshorts, Jonah makes it to the other side on one breath. He comes up to the surface amongst the splashing and horseplay. The strong smell of chloramines burns his nose as he catches his breath. Climbing up the ladder, the cool air chills his wet body. He stands in the warm sun, lets water drip from his bathing suit, to cool the hot concrete that burns his feet. As soon as his feet cool, he races across the blistering surface, heading for the deep end. A whistle blares, startling him. "No running!" shouts the lifeguard from his poolside tower. Afraid to look up, Jonah slows his pace and hustles on his heels and toes.

After reaching the ten foot mark, he pushes through the older kids who stand along the edge, waiting for their turn to cannon ball splash friends. As he dips his hot feet into the soothing water, someone yells, "Faggot!"

Jonah is secretly intrigued by the word scribbled in bathroom stalls. But hateful threats also warn him to stay clear of the poisonous indication that sometimes pushes innocent kids to the edge. Who's the unlucky boy now? Which bully does he need to also avoid? Jonah looks up a second too late and never sees who shoves him. Knocks the wind out of his chest and throws off his balance. He can't breathe and falls into the pool. Everything goes coldly dark.

. . .

Recovering consciousness, Jonah vomits water and struggles to breathe. Someone pushes him onto his side and he coughs up more liquid. His chest hurts, forcing him to take small quick breaths which drone out the ringing in his water-clogged ears. He rests a few minutes, breathing eases, and his mind reconnects with his wiry body. Feels his arms and legs again.

Rolls onto his back, blinks his eyes open, and attempts to see. Blurred movement and shadow. Jonah rubs his eyes and tries to focus, and in the penetrating light, the lifeguard comes into view—his green irises anxious; his hazel face and dark hair gleaming wet. Jonah has never been this close and vulnerable to an older boy before, and surely not one so good-looking. Time accelerates. Every passing minute, every breath, crowd into the next. The lifeguard's constricted pupils breach Jonah's defenses. He knows!

Breaking through the tense moment, his words finally reach Jonah's ears. "Por la gracia de Dios." He repeats them and sounds relieved. Kisses the small gold cross he wears around his neck. Puts his hand on Jonah's shoulder and leans closer. "You were lying at the bottom. I dove in and pulled you out of the water." He waits for Jonah to process the news. "You were unconscious, so I gave you CPR. Lucky you came around. . ." Accents his English to sound upbeat. "Rest now. The ambulance will be here pronto."

Jonah is, unaware of the gawking teens around him, is too busy visualizing the lifeguard pulling him onto the ledge, forcing his open mouth onto his. Repeatedly kissing him. Saving his life! Caught in a rip current of fear and desire, Jonah wants to look into those bright green eyes and ask him his name. Wants to thank him. Mostly, he wants to kiss him back. Afraid to say anything, he nods, but it is too late. He's stayed in his imagination too long.

"Look!" someone shouts. "Jonah has a boner!" Laughter erupts.

Jonah looks down at the protrusion in his trunks. Mortified, his eyes shift back to the lifeguard. "You should have let me drown," he insists, quickly getting up.

Shoving his way past the other teens, holding back tears, he races for the nearest exit, afraid to look back. Not long after the pool gate has closed behind him, Jonah pushes against the pain to find his second wind.

—

12

Eucalyptus Tree

Thinking back on the whole incident left Jonah with new regret and he kicked himself again for not getting the guy's name or having any courage at the time to say thanks. Trapped under so much fear, it took the whole next year for Jonah to find the nerve to go swimming again, and by then it had proven to be too late—the lifeguard had quit. Jonah figured he was the reason.

Four years later and he still couldn't let Green Eyes go, convinced by his heart that the guy was somewhere nearby, waiting. This unfinished obsession kept Jonah searching for him online, at school events, and around town. Every morning while getting dressed, told himself, today's the day I'll find him. Maybe at the mall or fast-food counter? Whatever it takes. . . He needed to thank him for saving his life and apologize for what happened. Crushing on him hard pushed Jonah to accept his queer tendencies. He'd made up his mind. Neither his parents nor the Reverend could pressure him now into believing that his attraction to boys needed a cure.

Jonah brought up the selfie of Jael and him on his phone. He couldn't wait to hang out with his new friend and couldn't wait to tell her what happened with his parents. "Thanks for saving my hide," he said to her face then set his phone on the ground.

Jonah admired his new tattoo again, it gave him superpowers, but knew he'd have to wash it off later. When he stood up to stretch—something else caught his eye. Carved into the tree were testaments of love and also militant shouts of hate. Below a poorly carved swastika someone wrote, 'God is white' and 'Lock 'em up!' Pairs of initials joined with a plus claimed the next space but Jonah didn't recognize their names and moved on. He continued around the tree, then stopped abruptly, his tongue stuck in his throat. '*Kill Fags*' was written in red spray paint. The hater communicating the urgency with heavy, slanted strokes.

Picking up a rusty bottle cap, he used the serrated edge to scrape off the hatred. In the empty space he scratched 'JL'. Above his initials, he carved 'GE'. Between them went a plus sign. More determined, he then went to work on the symbol for love; his cramped fingers pushing the cap into bark and gouging away wood with headstrong defiance. Not taking any chances, when the heart encircled them, he pierced it with fate's skyward arrow. When he was done, his face was red with vindication, and after shaking out his tired arm, Jonah spat his resentment onto the ground. The secret he fought so hard to protect was now exposed. His first promise of love that he hoped—way out here—would survive. Safe from unwanted attention and online social venom. Seeing their bound initials was enough validation. His way of saying thanks.

Sitting against the tree, Jonah pulled off his sneakers and stuffed his smelly socks inside each shoe. He slipped his phone into his cargo shorts pocket then headed down to the water.

Walking through the cool splash was an incredible distraction in the hot sun but it still couldn't stop his over-thinking. Jonah pictured his parents counseling with the Reverend and scheming against him. He knew they'd have his packed suitcase waiting. Go for treatment or be kicked out of the house.

Jonah imagined getting into a white van—a rideshare for ruined kids, with locked doors, bolted steel partition, tinted windows. Being entertained the entire drive with a Hellfire and Brimstone video sermon that would have some kids crying by the time the closing facility gates locked them inside. Imagined countless brainwashing sessions, and even harsher punishments, until he drank their Kool-Aid and danced with Jesus out the front door. College money well spent.

Another thought terrified him more. What if their remedies failed to make him straight? What then? His phone buzzed—startling him back to reality. Jael's text helped him shake off his nerves, and he excitedly headed back, knowing she was nearly here.

Jonah took a shortcut across the sand, climbed up the embankment and made it into the shade when he stepped on something sharp. Jonah groaned, lifted his foot, and pulled a large thorn out of his heel. It was curved and sharp and black. Eyeing the barb, he quipped 2 Corinthians 12:7. "To keep me from becoming proud, I was given a thorn in my flesh, a messenger of Satan, to torment me."

Quickly realizing what it was, Jonah dropped onto his knees, set the talon beside him and carefully ran his fingers through the warm sand. Up came a thin splintered bone. He started to dig and not more than a foot down—found the bird's macabre remains.

"Way cool…"

He used a stick to probe the pile of bones and followed the line of vertebrae to where they disappeared. The stick felt something hard. He scraped away more earth. Blew at the sand and uncovered a skull. Even in death the bird seemed alive—its large eyeholes staring with intent—and broad ebony beak waiting to strike.

"Talk of the Devil, and he's bound to appear—" Jonah remarked but cut himself off when he spotted something else poking through the bones. He pulled gently on the reed and the deadly arrow revealed itself—five inches long, with a triangular, steel blade at its apex. He spun the shaft with his fingers and the lethal metal signaled with sunlight. Easing the broken shaft into his side pocket, Jonah buttoned the flap, then placed the claw and bone back into the hole and filled it with sand. When he was satisfied the grave was hidden, he limped down to the water to wash his heel, and then went to get his shoes.

Sitting on a small log, Jonah used his sock to wipe sand from his injured foot, and inspected his heel. The puncture was crusted with red grains which he washed off with water from his bottle before gulping the rest.

"Best day for a swim," said a girlish voice.

Jonah recognized Jael's parlance and threw a friendly smile over his shoulder but all he could see was the hood that came down over his head. His arms were jerked and he blindly stumbled to find his feet. He tried to break free and fought back. His own resistance and heavy breathing competed with the sound of traveling shoes that dragged him through the sand.

Minutes later he was being spun around and dizzily begged for the prank to stop. Someone pushed him backwards, slamming his back against the tree, ropes bit his wrists and his shoulders pitched forward as his arms were drawn around the trunk behind him.

—

13

Trout

When the hood came off, the world was still spinning, and Jonah had to close his eyes and concentrate on breathing to keep from throwing up. Once the motion stopped, he saw three older boys break from their huddle and form an offensive line.

"Looks like we've caught us a fish," one of them said, rubbing his palms together.

The two other boys agreed.

Jonah knew them immediately, not by their names, but by their orange laced red sneakers and, wresting against the ropes, Jonah played his only hand.

"My friend will be here any minute."

The first boy laughed. "Hey, Jael! You can come down now."

Seconds later, Jael ambled down the embankment in a GOD Squad halter top and tight jeans, cracking a mischievous smile as she tucked her halo-blond hair behind her ear.

Jonah knew something was wrong when her red shoes snagged his awareness. "Hey Jael, what's going on?"

Jael flashed him a smirk as she approached. "I wanted to call you Rainbow but they said it was too obvious."

Jonah ignored the boys' snickers. "Seriously, am I being pranked?"

"Since you biked all the way out here, I'll be nice, and introduce my posse. We're all here for you," she grinned. Then stepped to Jonah's side and pointed to an inked, buzz cut blond. "Meet Cade."

Cade pulled up his sleeve and flashed his swastika-locked cross tattoo.

Jonah was relieved that the dragonfly on his arm was hidden against the Eucalyptus.

"Tuck," Jael said next, "come say hi to Trout."

The red haired guy lit a cigarette then came forward. He blew smoke rings into Jonah's face from behind his mirrored shades, made the sound of dripping water with his voice, and quietly walked away.

"And that steroid Neanderthal," Jael fingered, "is my BF, Tovy."

Tovy showed off his muscled guns.

Jonah's voice shook as he uttered, "I thought you were my friend."

"You told me you didn't have any, remember?" Her patronizing smile grew as she put her hand down her pants. "I bet you've never smelled a girl before," she said. "Maybe you're not really queer?" Pulling out her hand, she placed her fingers up to his nose and then traced them over his lips.

Jonah locked eyes with hers and refused to react.

"Its official, guys," she looked back at her friends, disappointed. "Trout doesn't like girls." Jael turned her attention back on Jonah. "Give a guy fish, you feed him for a day." She raised her soiled fingers together, "But teach him how to fish, and he'll eat for a lifetime." Grinning, she made a V sign, pressed her fingers up to her mouth and flicked her tongue. She sashayed over to Tovy. "Tell me, Trout. Have you ever given a guy head? Girls rule when they hold a guy's dragon by the balls." She didn't wait for Jonah's answer. "Want me to show you how? The trick. . . don't forget to breathe through your nose." She fumbled to undo Tovy's jeans. "It never takes him long," she remarked, inadvertently snagging his zipper.

"Sixty-second assassin," cracked Tucker with his cigarette wedged between his lips.

Jonah quietly worked his wrists to try and free himself.

Tovy shot both middle fingers at his friends then grabbed Jael's arm. He freed his zipper and pulled it up. "Stay focused," he stroked her hair. "That storm on the horizon is moving in fast. I need you to go get the boat like we planned."

Jael smirked and saved him with a peck on the lips. "You're saddlebacking me later." She made her order clear by squeezing his crotch as she departed.

Cade threw a questioning look at Tucker.

"Up the ass," mouthed Tuck.

"Don't be tripping over each other's dicks while I'm gone…" She huffed as she climbed the slope and headed for the woods.

"Hey, Jael?" Cade and Tucker excitedly called to her.

"No, you boys can't watch. Pervs!" She yelled back, taking her smile with her.

When she was gone, the boys converged on Jonah.

Jonah tried to reason with the group, "Please just let me go. I won't tell anyone. I promise."

Tovy shook his head, "We can't just let you off the hook, Trout."

"Good one, Tovy," remarked Tucker.

"Hell no!" Cade jumped in. "We can't have a try hard, mama's boy perv running round."

Jonah knew it was time to fight back, be like them, then maybe the boy's wouldn't see him as a threat and let him go. He eyed Cade. "Ignorance is a popular meal for kids with dirty nails."

"Ouch! You just got burned dude." Tuck popped Cade with the back of his hand.

Cade, red-faced, anxiously picked at the dirt under his nails. "You know it's our goddamn civic responsibility to kick your ass."

Jonah watched Cade's dirty fingers rub a dirtier fist.

"It says so in the Bible," said Cade. "Even the Devil knows it." He charged Jonah but Tovy stopped him.

"Hold on boys!" Tovy pushed Cade back. "I am an assassin…" He gazed up into the tree and then turned his eyes on the lake. "TC, you guys are not gonna believe this. Four years ago, I watched Trout get baptized…right out there." Tovy strutted up to Jonah. "I actually did you a favor that day. I barebowed an old Devil's crow right out of this tree."

Jonah studied Tovy's lit face and knew what he'd done but said nothing.

"I remember the damn thing wouldn't stop squawking… *Just like you.*" Tovy made his point, poked his finger in Jonah's chest, and grinned when he noticed the tiny bump beneath Jonah's shirt.

Jonah didn't know what to think when Tovy's finger drew circles around his nip.

"I bet you're on some queer hookup app exchanging dick pics," whispered Tovy. His voice carried a suggestion of envy, but scoffs from his friends, stiffened him into pinch-twisting the tiny flesh.

Jonah winced and tried to jerk away.

"There Trout goes, squawking again. I thought queers liked it rough. How about the other one?"

But before Tovy could pinch the other, Jonah's knee landed in Tovy's groin.

"That's the spirit!" Tovy thrilled and grabbed Jonah by his throat. "I can take it like a man. Now it's your turn. . ."

Jonah felt Tovy's knee press against his own.

"Open your mouth like a good fish."

When Jonah opened his mouth, Tovy hawked up a loogie and spit then pushed Jonah's chin closed. "Now swallow."

Jonah closed his eyes and tried not to think about what traveled down his throat.

"By the way, karma's a bitch!" said Tovy.

When Tovy's knee returned the favor, Jonah lost his breath. Inconceivable pain attacked his groin, traveled up his abdomen, and knotted his stomach. His roped arms held him up.

Tucker and Cade cupped their junk and grimaced.

Tovy walked away with a big smile. "Cade, you're up to bat."

"Good, because I have an itch!" The blond boy was ready.

"There's a pill for that!" joked Tucker as his friend passed.

Jonah gave a pleading look at the zit-faced kid who was about his size and watched him pace around, nervously preoccupied.

"When I was nine," said Cade, "coach Randall asked me to help him one day after school. Said he he'd pay me. So I followed him into the locker room. No one around but us…" Cade shoved Jonah hard against the tree. "He pushed me against the cinderblock wall." Cade creased his oily, red face at Jonah, "But now I know how to throw a punch."

The blow sent Jonah's face to the side and before he could recover, Cade threw his other fist in the name of the Almighty. It wasn't the punch that hurt, it was the pain of knowing that he was the next queer in line—taking a beating—because ignorance and hardened public opinion, granted them self-righteous permission.

Cade squeezed Jonah's bloodied mouth. "I'll pay the ferryman to take you both to hell… so I can sit back, eat popcorn and watch the Devil tail-fuck you while you burn…" He pushed Jonah's face aside and fumed away, rubbing his bruised, grubby knuckles.

Tucker handed Cade his last smoke along with some passing advice. "Dude you've got to quit getting high and binge-watching horror flicks."

Cade blew him off.

Jonah spit blood from his cut mouth as Tucker approached and flicked his cigarette at him. The sound of dripping water teased Jonah's sanity.

"I'm no one. Why do you want to hurt me?"

"You want to know why??" Tucker questioned. His ginger face

was sweating as he grabbed a handful of Jonah's hair and nodded his head yes. "Alright..." he smirked. "You were born cursed and have no heaven. Got something to say about it?" he asked before popping Jonah's head against the tree.

Heat shimmers across the hot sand and Jonah thinks he is dreaming when light rays bend into movement. He strains to see over Tucker's shoulder. A feminine silhouette approaches. White, high heel boots crunch in the sand. Her summer dress is couture and modish. A chin-length bob and blunt-cut bangs frame her dramatic, feathered-lash, eyes and red carpet lips. Her face is beautiful. Jonah can't take his eyes off her.
"I liked your joke about drag queens and church," her low voice says.
Jonah is embarrassed. "Where did you come from?"
"Like you, from a sacred place, where only the bravest find themselves." Her eyes smile. "We all stand with you," she says along with others.
Jonah is surrounded by a community of strangers with different ethnicities.
"Together we hold the line..." She leans in close. "Let me gift you some understanding." Whispers something in his ear and gently lifts his chin with her large, nail polished, fingers.
"I couldn't hear you. What did you say?" He tries to ask, but when Jonah blinks, she and the others are gone.

His defiant eyes turn to Tucker. "My right to be isn't yours to make. And love's understanding doesn't answer to a faith. Or—"

"You dumb fuck!" Tucker cut him off.

Jonah caught his deliberate southern drawl and cigarette breath and winced as his hair was pulled tighter.

"The problem with you high-minded libs..." scoffed Tucker. "You think conservatives and patriots still come from a low tide gene pool in Appalachia. Here's your new reality. We're white, conservative, educated. Love guns more than God. We're taking back this rotting country…town by town." Tucker's disgust showed on his teeth. "Cleaning house…"

Jonah tasted his vinegar and deep-rooted hate. When he looked away, Tucker's face followed him and Jonah saw his own pummeled face looming in Tucker's mirrored lenses.

"Our political fight is just getting started," Tucker warned, removing his shades.

For the first time, Jonah could see his upside down eyes pressed against his flattened auburn brow.

"Queer fish should know better than to swim in backwaters." Tucker pointed his fingered gun at Jonah's head. "It's where boys like you disappear. *Pop!*" His hand fired.

Jonah thought it was thunder when his head hit the tree again and shifted his eyes skyward. As he recited the Lord's Prayer, clouds fell in meteoric drops and burst with slow-motion into millions of ricocheting marbles. Then the sky melted into blue lines that shrieked down the atmosphere with teeth-gnashing screams. Water rushed in, life liquefied around him, and everything swirled together into rising black paint.

—

14

Nina

Jonah's vision comes and goes as pain rattles his brain, and when he can finally see, he is standing among hundreds of bounding fans impatiently screaming for the concert finale. Their pandemonium hits him like a shockwave, absorbs the hurt and built-up pressure in his head, as if by a miracle, sets him free.

He pushes through the dancing crowd of Gen Z's. So many girls of every race, shape and size, celebrating their collective independence with dyed hair and glitter makeup. Hidden among them, are groups of queer boys, being comfortable and affectionate, and now knows why his parents wouldn't let him come.

Passing through a raucous squad brings a pinch to his butt. Jonah quickly moves on and eventually finds a spot closer to the laser lit stage. The energy is palpable. Moments later everything goes dark. The arena falls into quiet with collective anticipation.

Somewhere in the darkness a cello begins playing heavy, veiled notes with rising intensity and the Milky Way spirals onto the main stage projection screen. Thunderous flashes shake the arena, frightening some teens into grabbing their friends, but others jump with excitement.

Slow at first then faster, stars speed off the screen, fly out into the arena, winning collective sighs. Soon they are traveling at light speed to *the cello's marching movement and Jonah is awed by purple clouds of illuminated dust and gas.*

Many fans record the enthralling scene with their phones and some teens even try catching stars with their reaching hands.

Entering the Orion Spur, spectators race near colossal Jovian Gods: Neptune, Uranus, Saturn and Jupiter, and continue towards the small copper sphere in the distance.

Somersaulting through space, the next thing Jonah knows, they are plummeting down to the Red Planet's surface. Flying across the wasteland of littered volcanic rock, along riverbeds of oxidized iron dust and through storms. Following the quickly rising landscape, everyone gasps when they drop into an expansive caldera and then catapult up into the cosmos.

Watching the rusting planet diminish in rear view, Jonah wonders if Mars, the Roman god of war, is attempting to warn us of our awaiting fate from his plinth in the Pantheon. He has little time to give it more thought seeing the video shift focus onto the small blue planet ahead.

The cello eases into a harmonic cantilena. A kick drum detonates without warning and Earth jumps closer. A second heavy beat brings the audience closer still and then comes a third and the crescent blue Earth looms; majestic and exposed.

Tapping drumsticks count off the seconds to go. Out of time, the drummer unleashes them on his drums and the Earth explodes into confetti raining over the crowd.

Jonah manages to catch a falling disc which has a lenticular, 3D image of the word 'REVOLUTION!' held up by arms of protesting youth —that when viewed from a different angle says 'VOTE'.

Roaming spotlights converge center stage. Pushing to see, Jonah catches sight of the frontwoman rising up from a floor trap, sending thousands of fans into total pandemonium.

Dressed in bohemian cool, rocking a black vinyl jacket and chopped Afro blue hair, Nina tries reaching for the mic but is stopped by red neon ropes that tether her wrists to the platform.

Fighting against her restraints, she strains her thin body forward, forces her purple colored lips onto the mic, and then turns her glam eyes at the bright lights. She takes the moment to let the world's injustice bare its heavy weight upon her; channel her strength; motivate and inspire.

Summoning her siren, she waits until the fiery bird is flapping in her throat. Inhaling hard, she sets it free through her quivering lips, singing a cappella, "No more…"

The video reverses to bring destroyed Earth back to life and Nina sing's to the Mermen's slow playing tempo.

Images of driving seas and ancient forests give Jonah chills.

Rippled dunes transition to an oasis of palms and ferns. A bitten apple rolls onto the mossy ground. Slithering around the eaten fruit, a ruby-eyed green viper lifts its head and tastes the air with its flicking tongue. Drawn to sounds of humans fucking, the snake grins and races off in their direction.

Eve screams in labor and Adam pisses soldier ants that march across the continents. Their colonies rise into kingdoms and ants into armies of men.

Red sand falls rapidly through a modern hourglass and the apprehensive mood is riven by a guitar lick. Pounding drums, smoke and strobing lights signal conflict, and with raw emotion, Nina wails against the backdrop of modern-day warfare.

Missiles hiss in flight. Terrified people run for their lives with cell phones to their ears. A blinding light flashes and when the smoke clears, people are gone. Generals congratulate themselves while soaking in a steaming bath of what looks like blood.

Discarded among burned out vehicles and bombed buildings, the city's former brilliance is pictured on a page in a travel magazine. A young Asian man closes the journal and slides it inside his briefcase. As he steps out into the haze, he opens an umbrella and disappears into the hustling crowd of umbrellas.

A military analyst remotely tracks his movement on several screens while fisheye surveillance cameras record street activity. Monitors list everyone by name and social rank. Red sand continues falling through the timepiece.

Burning into the chorus, Nina trills over an amplified guitar hook. Thousands in the arena sing along, but Jonah doesn't know the words, and keeps his wide eyes on the jumbotron's grainy video of perahan tunban wearing men digging a hole near a pile of stones. Not long for the world, a young girl desperately pulls on her ropes.

Dropping into her raspy lower register, Nina channels her rage, belting out, "Hegemonic oppression calls for change. Give us resolve to break their chains!" Thrusting up her fists, airbursts of light and smoke and fireworks erupt, severing both their restraints. She grabs the mic and sings hard as the Mermen rock the song in high gear.

The freed girl stands defiant and faces her executioners. The men turn their backs and mortar their stones onto a wall. The wall becomes a school. She is handed a book. A tribal leader opens the door and she walks inside. Seconds later, an educated woman appears in the doorway. Optimism shows on her scarred face.

As she walks along a dirt road, the crumbling village comes to life, evolving into a prospering town. Stopping to look around, the town rises into a capital around her, and the road becomes a hallway.

Walking on, she approaches the guarded door at the end of the corridor. The header sign reads, 'Nations of Women Council'. She enters. Another county on the world map turns purple, eliciting applause throughout the stadium.

Taking off her jacket, Nina removes the mic and marches across the stage, powering into the song's bridge, quavering, "Governments of corruption! Apocalypse of our destruction! Dissidents are silenced birds! When political gavels over-turn, our right to be will disappear. Mother Earth has cried all her tears…"

Running back to center, sliding onto her knees, Nina beseeches the spirit of the great Native American chief tattooed onto her lesbian back. Crying out his name, "Hin mah too yah lat kekt!"

Pointing up at the sacred eagle feather on the concert screen, she implores her fans, "Stand up while power is yours and sing with me… No more!" Rising with the audience, she sings her message again and again, and the feather becomes a quill. Writing, 'No more injustice' in several languages.

Taking over center, the green-hair lead guitarist plays through the melody, shreds galvanizing riffs, and cuts improvisational breakdowns under the hot strobing lights.

Massive yellow 'AI' letters move freely on screen, then become trapped inside a shrinking red circle, until 'AI' movements are tightly controlled.

Images appear so fast that Jonah is afraid to blink.

Racial violence and civil unrest. Protests for Independence and democratic reform. Government retaliation. Hard to watch public whippings. Hangings and executions. A protestor's self-immolation.

Political rallies and online posts, the word Conspiracy and Fake News! Black men looking through prison bars. Children crying behind fencing. Confederate statues falling and rioters storming the Capital.

Women marching. Blacks marching. Queers marching. Latinos marching. Indigenous people follow.

A powerhouse of lesbians stand together for change. Teens collectively use T-shirts to explain their identities: she-transgender, him-non-binary, we-intersex, and fluid. Their fierce determination leaves Jonah saddened at his own lack of courage.

The band jams out a breakdown to visuals of animated violence.

A video game AK rifle searches for the target in its cross-hairs. A white-handed puppet master dangles a ballot box above reaching arms of color. 'FEAR' trembles into view followed by 'HATRED'. The first five letters huddle together, vote out the letter D and the word 'DISCRIMINATE', spelled with icons of weaponry, pinwheels away. The remaining letters quickly trade places, spelling 'HEART' which grows larger with each beat until the screen is red. There's a collective sigh.

Red becomes a homeless woman's tattered jacket. She shuffles past an unconscious addict, screams at him to stop using his mind to touch people, and is mentally oblivious to the 'MISSING PERSON' flyer of her posted on a nearby light pole, or the security robot that patrols by.

Images of Mega mansions and superyachts loom and then a box of segregated crayons spills onto the screen. They quickly melt together.

Joining in, the rhythm player frets broken chords with harmonic progressions as religious symbols flash by.

People of faith worshiping. Religious places follow: Lourdes, France. Kashi Vishwanath Temple. Mahabodhi Temple. Mecca. Mount Sinai, Egypt. Uluru-Kata Tjuta National Park. Modern cities come next: Kremlin. Beijing. London. Paris. Tokyo. Seoul. Istanbul. Hong Kong. Dubai. Pyongyang. Kuala Lumpur. Bangkok. Sydney. New York. San Francisco.

Sitting at the piano, Nina's fingers work the keys, letting inspiration take her through improvisational runs, chasing a musical high. "I love you, Octavia!" Nina tells her cellist lover through her mic, to the delight of her fans, and then points to the keyboardist who comes in on synthesizer—shifting the song into a heavy, industrial grind.

Glaciers are melting. Seas rise. Lakes rapidly evaporate and fires rage. A massive barge dumps trash into the sea. Waves of plastic wash up on a beach. Trees fall and a young mountain gorilla looks on with worry. From space, Earth appears scorched and bilious. The hourglass is nearly out of sand.

Reaching crescendo, Nina and the Mermen rock into the final chorus. Everyone in the stadium is on their feet, waving their arms and singing. Seeing lyrics on screen, Jonah sings too.

Falling through the hourglass
World's turned upside down
Trapped inside, old men contrive
To keep their powerhouse
Blood and bones keep piling up
Raise your voices loud
Or risk losing everything
In Adam's playground

A stage curtain opens and his church choir emerges. Led by Director Burns, add their harmonic voices and shaking tambourines to the cause.

Victims of oppression, violence and state sanctioned punishment appear alongside champions for human rights. As their images contract, they fill empty spaces on a round grid, leaving one vacancy.

Jonah's own face appears. Seeing his picture fall into the spot leaves him ashamed and embarrassed. He doesn't know that kid. Can't think of a sacrifice or personal achievement beyond the queer appellation painted on his high school locker.

The circle spins rapidly. Becomes a sphere. Constricts into a glowing, turquoise healing stone that drops inside the timekeeper by the chief's mystical hand.

Sliding her mic back into the stand, Nina pours all of her hope and love into the universe. Catches flashes of her fans' crying faces before time runs out. When she throats the final refrain there comes no sound. Seized by panic, she tries again, still no sound. There's no music in her in-ear monitor.

She hears the audience's collective gasp and quickly looks up at the screen behind her. Her watery eyes struggle to adjust to the changing light. Her face beads sweat. Eventually finding the pile of red sand at the bottom, she moves her focus higher and sighs too. Feeling the chief's immortal power, her upturned eyes release their tears. The glowing stone is lodged in the glass neck holding back time. Her emotional expression suddenly appears on the jumbotron, and seeing herself, she can no longer move.

Jonah looks around the stadium and quickly realizes everyone is perfectly still, except him. He turns for the nearest exit, but movement in the crowd catches his attention. "Hey! Do you know what's going on?"

The person stops, turns around and lowers his white hoodie. "What's up, Jonah?" Jesus is the same age as he is in the living room mural.

"Wait! Is it really you?" Jonah doesn't give him time to answer. "What are you doing here?"

"They're a great band. They rock and their songs inspire."

"Millions around the world worship you...why are you not helping us?"

"I've tried, but you fail to listen. You fail the planet and most importantly, you continually fail to love each other."

"And that's why we need you. I need you…"

"Don't be disheartened. Hold out your hand and I'll show you something cool."

Jonah reluctantly holds up his palm.

Jesus fires up his vape pen which looks more like a tiny musical instrument and sets the light to yellow. Taking a short hit, he exhales curried smoke that transitions into a dragonfly. The insect draws circles in the air then lands on Jonah's palm to groom itself. Without warning, the creature plunges its tail into Jonah's flesh, and in the few seconds it takes him to pull back his hand, the dragonfly dissipates. Leaving Jonah with the horror of watching a hatched nymph creep under his skin to the spot between his forearm veins.

"It is what we don't like about ourselves that leaves us in fear," says Jesus and then he explains the power of dragonflies. "Their iridescence is the mirror to introspection. Their eyes see the imaginable and their wings bear acceptance." Jesus gazes at Jonah with the same compassion from the hillside mural. "You already figured this out."

That long awaited validation brings Jonah to tears which he quickly wipes away.

Switching the pen to blue and taking another toke, Jesus blows a smoke ring with a backspin that, instead of dispersing, forms a shaft of silvery blue that wiggles to life and swims in silhouette between them. The fish develops dark spotting and blush stripes, and Jonah thinks about using his newly found validation to ask Jesus if this is a cruel joke.

The trout dulls into bones and the bones into a sketch. The ichthus swims fast around him and comes close enough for him to see his waving hand through its intersecting arcs. When Jonah tries to pet the fish, like he sometimes does with his angel's, the ichthus swims off, leaving him and Jesus to watch it take a direct line through the fixed crowd.

"Fish always find their way," Jesus tells him. Says he has one more mystery to share and advises Jonah to step back. With the pen glowing white, the Messiah exhales three portentous clouds that join and blacken *into a great bird that then comes to life; its obsidian feathers catch more light than is really there.*

Jesus says ravens keep their eye on history. Enduring sentries that patrol the frontlines dividing light and shadow, virtuous and eerie, ignorance and understanding. Hold us accountable.

Jonah has to duck as the raven swoops over him and watches the creature escape out an open skylight.

"The concert is over, Jonah," says Jesus as the stadium lights come on and the audience returns to life. He backs into the crowd.

Jonah tries to follow him, pushing through the line of exiting kids, but there are too many. "Wait! I have to know what the fish...and the bird have to do with me."

"Time explains everything. Tell your mother. . ."

"Are you ever coming back? You have to tell me. Please!" But it is too late. Jesus is gone and so is the band and everyone else.

Jonah looks around at all the empty seats and then up at the skylight again. Hears his echoing answer, "I haven't decided..." Jonah slumps into an empty seat and tries to make sense of it all.

—

15

Red Shoes

The hard deck pressed against Jonah's back, pitched against the waves, and pulled him out of his dream. He remained perfectly still. Listened to his assailants bicker and caught tiny glimpses of their squeaky red sneakers moving around him.

"Guys, that storm is coming this way fast," Cade voiced his worry.

"Someone burnt God's toast and now he's really pissed!" joked Tucker.

Tovy checked his watch, "Time to get our fish in the water."

"I've got his shoes!" Tuck called dibs.

Jonah didn't flinch when his sneakers were yanked from his feet.

Tuck shoved them into his backpack, thrilled. "Another pair to hoist up the *fagpole*."

"Throw his socks in the water. He won't need them." Jonah heard Jael say. "And Cade…forget the damn storm, get the rope ready."

Tovy sat on top of Jonah and slapped his face until he opened his eyes.

"Welcome back. I bet you like waking up and finding me on top of you. Turning your crank, huh Trout?"

But Jonah was too distracted over discovering his bike on the boat.

Pissed over being ignored, Tovy reached behind him and grabbed Jonah's junk, "Buck up boy! That's what pa always tells me. . ."

Jonah groaned as Tovy squeezed.

"I thought you liked straight guys. Don't all queers?"

"You're not a lifeguard," quipped Tucker as he dropped to his knees and looked at Jonah upside down. "I was at the pool that day, but you probably don't remember. Who do you think pushed you?" His friends shared his laugh. "Tell you what, *Bonerboy*... I'm gonna help you out."

Chills and fear seized Jonah as Tucker ripped away his shirt and called for Cade. While Tovy and Cade held Jonah down, Tucker used part of his shirt to gag his mouth. Then retrieved his knife from his back pocket, held it up in Jonah's face, and pressed the trigger.

When the rusty blade flipped open, Jonah closed his eyes tight, and bit down hard on his shirt, but before he felt the blade against his forehead, he was running fast down the street—away from the pool again. Away from reality. But this time he wasn't fast enough. Someone tripped him to the ground. Tucker loomed.

"Now everyone will know you're queer," said Tucker, as he set his knife onto Jonah's bare chest. His finger picked up some warm blood which he smeared onto the carved mark on Jonah's forehead. "Triangles and queers below together, like those branded Nazi homos we read about in world history."

"Weren't those triangles pink?" questioned Tovy.

But before Tucker could jab back, Cade seized the opportunity and jumped up, feet together, as he gave a right arm salute. "Heil Hitler!"

Tucker stood too. "Are you fucking kidding me??" he asked

with insulting laughter that quickly turned acidic. "So now you're a dumbass skinhead or what? Our red shoes, ain't good enough for ya no more?"

Cade moved out of Tucker's shadow to cast his own over Jonah. "Maybe I'm tired of being your tool!" He stared down his friends. "Government keeps taking our rights...our jobs," his finger pointed at Jonah. "Giving them to blacks and bean pickers and *queers!*" This time, Cade refused to back down. "Someone's got to fight for our way of livin' and our history."

"Dude, we're in the same fight," reminded Tucker. *"Red Shoes!"*

"Red Shoes," everyone shouted at Cade. *"Red Shoes! Red Shoes!"*

Jonah saw his chance, grabbed the knife and threw it overboard, but before the weapon plopped into the water, the blade snagged Tovy's thigh.

"You sonofabitch!"

Jonah shook his head, tried to apologize through his gag, but all he saw was Tovy's fist.

—

16

Keeping Score

The athletic stadium is vacant as Jonah stands atop the scoreboard near the entrance to the high school track and field complex. Even the make out bleachers are empty. Eyeing the thirty-foot drop to the ground below, he carefully adjusts his bare feet on the narrow ledge extending twenty feet beyond his toes.

Jonah raises his arms parallel with the ground. Letting them teeter until he finds his balance. Slowly lifting his foot, he places it forward on the narrow footing of hot metal and carefully shifts his weight. With his first step taken, he takes a moment to breathe. Lifting his other foot sends his arms flailing and he wishes he'd given PE gymnastics the same attention he put into watching the other boys.

With a few more scary steps, Jonah finds his center of gravity, and is almost across when a whistle blares, nearly sending him off the ledge. Forcing himself to look down, he expects to find his coach on his phone talking with authorities. Prays for a suspension or to be kicked off the team. A voice says he might not get to graduate now, but only a robin patrols the grass below. Jonah checks the grounds again.

"Trout," says Tovy with a whistle in his mouth. "What are you doin' up here?"

"Get out of my way, Tovy!"

"Why are queers always trying to validate themselves?"

"Because we matter!" Jonah steps forward, forcing Tovy back. "To have the same right to love and place at the table... and so that scared, closeted boys don't have to think their only options are violence and suicide."

"Check the score, Trout. Four to one," Tovy snickers as he shoves Jonah, hard. "You cut me! Seems fair that you lose a tooth. Time to wake up, dreamer!"

As his balance fails, Jonah makes a desperate attempt to grab Tovy's shirt; his hand just missing the words: ★ AMERICAN BADASS MUSCLE ★ as Tovy steps back.

Falling, Jonah watches the scoreboard rise taller and Tovy, with his wicked grin, grow smaller. His forearm is bare but suddenly there's wiggling and the dragonfly reappears as the boat deck rises against his back.

—

17

Deep-Six

Jonah yanked himself out of his free fall right before impact; floundering on the deck like a caught fish. The gag was gone and his tongue quickly discovered the space between his molars. Then his adversaries came into focus. Cade and Tucker were up to something but he couldn't see around Jael, who was crouched next to Tovy.

"Look whose back…" Tovy intoned.

"Hold still!" Jael insisted as she pushed Tovy's wound apart. Blood ran down his thigh.

"You sure you know what you're doing, Jael?"

"I was a Junior Volunteer at the health clinic for two years. I've definitely seen worse." Jael explained, while she covered his wound with fresh gauze and a bandage. "Blood makes me lit, probably because I was a cutter in middle school." She tossed away the bloodied gauze that she used to stop the bleeding. It landed so close to Jonah, he could taste metal.

Tovy thanked her with a kiss and turned to Jonah as he buckled up his jeans. "You got me good, Trout. I'm really surprised you had the balls."

"I didn't mean for that to happen," Jonah tried to apologize.

Tucker's shadow fell upon him. "That was my great grandfather's knife. Damn good thing it's gone, or you wouldn't have a pair now."

Lightning shot over the lake with a tremendous blast, followed by more lightning, and more thunder and brought Cade out of hiding. "Guys, we need to get off this lake. Now!"

"Where's your faith, Cotter?"

Cade stared Jael down. "In my back pocket. Same as you…"

"God's doing right by me," she sassed back at him.

"Well, I know better than to test him."

"Or me…" She pushed him out of her way. "We're not going anywhere until we take the selfie."

"I'm ready," said Tucker. Pulling a fifth from his bag and removing the cap, he handed the whiskey to Jael. "Girls always start."

She swallowed a mouthful and shouted, "Ten!" Then passed the bottle over to Tovy.

Tovy took a hard drink and yelled, "Nine!" And tried to hand it over to Cade, who still had his attention on the rising storm.

"Fuckit!" said Cade, who doused his fears with alcohol and choked out, "Eight!"

Taking back his whiskey, Tucker drank like a pro, downed the rest then hollered, "Seven!"

The group made a hand stack over Jonah that erupted with everyone yelling, "Deep-Six the faggot!"

They used his shirt to blindfold him. Activity and whispers had him afraid. Then came movement—his arms and legs carrying all his weight—until they were released. His blinded hands broke his plunge into the rough, chilly water that took his breath. Jonah immediately fought his way to the surface and pulled the blindfold from his eyes. Shaking in the lake, he yelled up to his supposed friend, "Why, Jael?"

"You were next on the list."

Her answer left him guessing, and all he could do was watch

the boys pose as Jael took their selfie. A brief moment of sunshine hit him with warmth; last catches of sunlight glistened on the water and then disappeared. Life fell cold and dark and left him shivering against the rising wind and waves.

"Hey, Trout, we figured you'd want your stuff back!" Cade emptied the contents of his backpack over the side. His sketchbook made a small splash.

"Nice drawings by the way. *Oops!*" Tucker tossed Jonah's phone at him. "Your mother's been calling and calling!" he yelled. "You really should call her back!"

As Jonah thought about his mother, a rogue wave broke over his head and eclipsed his vision.

—

18

Mary

Jonah forces open his eyes. He is back at his desk. Nina's tearful face shows on his monitor. He sits up in his chair, more tired than usual, and realizes he'd been asleep. Lost in a dream of his own making. Hears his frustrated mother call his name again and presses the computer power switch. Nina disappears into black seconds before his mother bursts into his room.

"Time to pray, Jonah."

She is about to leave when Jonah feels something. The nymph is moving under his skin. He has to tell her even if she won't believe him, "Mama?"

"What now, Jonah?"

"I met the Messiah..."

His mother bristles and pretends not to hear.

"It's the truth," he insists.

She tries to shrug off his tale telling by looking away; pressing her lips flat and shaking her head. After a long minute of stewing, she closes the door and walks over, and kneels beside his chair. Her face is tense and unforgiving, "And just what did he say to you?"

"He asked me to give you a message."

"And why doesn't he tell me himself?"

"He's tried... But you're not listening. He said to tell you he loves you."

Her resentment melts into tears.

"Is this about me?"

His mother nods and explains that she regrets her life—that she never wanted to be married or have children. But peer pressure prevailed over abstinence and she got pregnant in high school. Living in a conservative town, the guilt and shame from having sex outside of marriage, became unbearable for her. She was called a fornicator and a whore by her own mother.

"And because I was seventeen, your grandparents threatened to have your father arrested if we didn't marry." She was forced out of school and forbidden to leave the house and couldn't have her friends over. "Your father flipped burgers after class and then we'd argue over the phone."

She finally allows herself to breathe. "I was so afraid that your father would leave me and every time I defended him, they threatened to kick me out. Every night I had to pray for forgiveness while they stood over me, listening, and then cry myself to sleep."

Jonah tries to comfort his mother but she pushes away his hand.

"We were married at city hall, and soon after... I miscarried your baby sister. Grandmamma said that her death was the Lord's punishment for conceiving her in sin. I believed her and that's when I became born again."

Jonah wonders why she treats him the same as her mother did her.

"When I got pregnant the second time, I prayed for another girl as His sign of forgiveness. But knew I wasn't in his graces when I saw the ultrasound. Your father beamed over you, but I worried myself, because you felt different." She takes a minute to prepare herself. "During your birth, I saw God standing behind the doctor, watching me. Terrified that he would also take you from us, I begged him no with every scream, refused to bring you into the world. When the doctor's scalpel cut you free, I wanted to suffocate your cries and hand your lifeless form to God as proof of my piety and penance fulfilled."

Jonah watches his mother wipe away her tears. "Mama... human *sacrifices, mercy killings, shame killings... can never bring honor or salvation. Abraham learned that with the Binding of Isaac."* He asks her why she doesn't love him.

"Because your birthday wish broke my heart and I helped you make it." She stops, unable to continue for some time. *"And then you went into my room and took what wasn't yours. Left me violated and embarrassed. You deserved that whipping."*

"Mama, why did you have those naked pictures under your mattress?"

"Your father quit showing up when he found out about you. Blamed me for being your accomplice. We played our parts, kept up the charade, but I was the reason for his miserable life and queer son. Those beautiful men made me feel wanted and desired. Gave me back control and self-worth. But they could never satisfy my need for love." She strokes Jonah's cheek. *"Or answer your heart either. I burned them in the fireplace when I was alone. Begged God for forgiveness and rededicated my life to faith. I thought if I could keep you straight, I'd save my marriage and make up for all my sins. So I burned them."* She hands him folded paper. *"But I didn't burn your Happy Ending."*

Jonah immediately recognizes his poem, his notice to God, his need for love. He pushes away all the hurt she's caused him. *"Mama, you've said many times that people make mistakes and not the Lord. We aren't meant to always understand His intentions or life's contradictions. Or to turn them into causes for a rightful afterlife. But what you can do... is let go of the guilt and shame that you hold over me and free yourself of your own. My being gay isn't keeping you out of heaven. That's Jesus's message."*

His mother gently brushes back Jonah's curly hair. *"Somebody needs a haircut."* She smiles bravely. *"I want to love you, Jonah. I want you to be happy. Find your love..."* Jonah clutches his mother close and bites his lip as tears wash away his hurt. Holds her even tighter when she tries to pull away.

"I have to go, now, son," she tells him. *"Always remember, 'All is fish that comes to his net.'"*

"What does it mean?"

"Make use of anything available," his mother insists. A moment later she is gone.

Jonah jumps from his chair and starts to run after her but somehow knows it is too late. He wipes away his tears, smiles at the paper and repeats, "All is fish that comes to his net." But as thunder booms, the paper, his words, his happily ever-after, disintegrates into sand. Water rises up to claim him. Jonah swims in every direction, but with try after try, can't breach the aquarium glass.

—

19

Reckoning

Jonah heard purrs and clicks, wiped water out of his face, and saw the boat moving in circles around him. It took all of his strength to tread the oncoming wake and swells. The sky was apocalyptic.

"You don't have much time, Trout," warned Tovy.

"Yea, better quit jerking off and start praying!" Cade pointed down at the water.

"Sinner's Lake is a good five miles in any direction," shouted Tucker. "Thought you might want to ride. Your tires are flat. Hope you brought a pump."

Jonah remembered seeing his bike onboard and realized a numbness in his foot. He fought against the water, pulled his leg to the surface, and discovered his sallow foot tied with rope. His fingers worked quickly to untie the knots—but none would ease.

"Remember, heaven's full, so try the basement," laughed Tucker.

"And you're gonna want a drink when you get there…" Cade hurled the emptied bottle of whiskey. It splashed down just beyond Jonah's reach.

"Anything you wanna confess, Trout?" Jael weighed in from

the driver's seat. "Thanks to you, Tovy will have a great scar story."

"Cut the flesh of every queer," Jonah shouted back. "We all bleed red not pink!" Rain started to ping the surface.

Everyone laughed at his confession. "Time to bounce!" hollered Tovy. The engine droned and the boat planed out of the water as raindrops quickened into a downpour.

—

20

400 m

Jonah knows this is going to be the hardest race of his life as he backs into the starting block and supports himself on his fingertips against the white line. Running the 400 m dash in the State Finals has always been a distant dream, wishful thinking, a thing with feathers. Making it through the trials has earned him this spot, but to prove his right to be here, he needs to cross the finish first. He lifts his hips and waits for the gun, and when it fires, drives out of the block low and fast. Legs and shoes pass him but he keeps with the pack. Burning more fuel, he advances into fourth, can easily take the lead, but running rabbit this early might leave him puking in the grass.

Keeping rapid pace, the pack of blurred forms shift around Jonah through the first 100 m. Everyone sucks down air and mentally accepts their next agonizing stride. Their unbearable labor becomes choreographed slow motion movements of choice.

Into the second turn, Jonah is third in the stagger, and in good position to ease the tension, and mentally prep for his burn down the backstretch. Distant cheering reaches his ears. He thinks about his parents sitting up in the stands. Are they clapping and calling his name? Stakes are higher today with so much on the line. Jonah knows he has to take the title to overcome all the disappointment they brought with them.

Running past the 200 m mark, he focuses on the upcoming turns. His lungs sear, his stomach wants to heave, his legs churn lactic acid. It's break or bail. At the 250 m mark, he swallows his sick, goes on the attack, asks for more hurt.

He races down last 100 m, moves up into second position, narrows the gap between him and the frontrunner. This is his shot, his one opportunity, to tell everyone to get out of his way. But the harder he kicks and pumps his arms—the slower he seems to move. He is too close to the lead, too close to victory to fall behind now. His neck strains and arms flail, but his body feels more metal than muscle, then his legs go missing. He doesn't feel his feet twist or his body yield to the track or skin peel away. Slowly lifts himself, moans in anguish, and sees the lead runner cross the finish. The other athletes pass him for roadkill as he dry heaves.

"Hey skinny kid?" His coach calls to him.

Jonah forces himself to sit up, still fighting to breathe, sees the ball cap wearing man standing in the sun.

The coach takes a knee beside him. "Don't be hard on yourself. You gave it your all and had everyone believing. Bonking comes with inexperience. The wall prepares you..." He puts his hand on Jonah's shoulder. "Sometimes losing is more consequential than winning."

But Jonah is distracted by something tugging on his shoe—his untied laces are cemented into the track. A heaviness is pulling on him. He remembers to check his arm. Sweat nor rain can wash away its verity. He thanks the dragonfly with a hard kiss, inhales his last breath, and closes his eyes.

—

21

Answers

Drowning in some ways, thought Jonah, was the same as running the 400 m. You've got to be in it to win it. You just can't breathe. There's thrashing and kicking and hurling limbs across the finish or realizing defeat seconds before passing out.

Sinking towards his inevitable fate, Jonah remembered what his mother had told him. Use anything you can. He acted quickly, but pulling on the rope only sent him deeper. Driven to find something he could use, Jonah swept his hands through the water, but felt only the passing current through his fingers.

His eyes stung from the churning flow. His lungs demanded air. He tried pushing his last breath back down his throat, back into his hungry lungs, but couldn't swallow. The shock was too much to withstand and his inner-self pulled away, and like removing dirty clothes—Jonah slipped out of his body.

When Jonah opened his eyes again, time moved in intervals around him, with leaves flitting in the wind and waves skipping like stones across the lake. He was soaked but his body didn't hurt and he felt metaphysically grounded, sitting on a bough in the old Eucalyptus tree. When he realized his distance to the ground, not taking any chances, Jonah grabbed onto an adjacent limb.

Nearby voices caught his attention. Aware of the gathering congregation, Jonah asked, "Who's the unlucky soul this time?" He craned for a better view and spotted his younger self standing head down next to his parents while they conversed with the deacons—unaware of the momentary shadow. The ominous bird nearly threw him off balance when it flapped down onto the bough. Jonah quickly shifted closer to the massive, mottled trunk to give the bird more space.

Folding its broad wings like scissors onto its back, the raven leaped within striking range, pinned him against the tree, and crooked its head to focus its pellet eyes on Jonah.

"*Kraa! Kraa! Kraa! Kraa! Kraa!*"

He had to cover his ears from the unpromising shrills.

When the cawing stopped, the bird bobbed its head and spoke. "Simul Justus et Peccator…" a feminine voice trilled.

"What??"

"Simul Justus et Peccator. . ." Her black eyes gleamed.

Jonah was left shaking his head and apologized. "First semester Spanish."

"Simultaneously justified righteous and a sinner," said the raven. "Principle of Martin Luther, Europe. 16th-century."

"Please tell me that I'm not crazy. That life hasn't left me running scared in death's video game, where fiends and beasts…" Jonah hesitated, "and birds feast upon the fallen."

"Saint and sinner. You are one and the same."

"If you're not here to take my eyes, then who are you?"

"An acolyte," said the raven. "Every soul has one." The bird throated a series of clicks then turned its attention to events on the ground.

Jonah watched too as his parents handed him over to the two elders and allowed the men to strip him of his clothes.

Time skipped forward and Jonah saw himself standing on the black box and asked the raven where he went wrong.

"You were chosen."

"Okay, now you're pranking me."

"Your gift comes with great consequence."

"You mean liability."

"You are as intended."

"You mean queer?"

"Extraordinary," claimed the raven.

"Why me?" he insisted. "I deserve the truth. Because every day I feel more alone than the day before. Getting hassled at school and sent texts urging me to kill myself. Every day from the day I knew, I've tried to fight it and deny it, but can't. These feelings won't let go and praying isn't working or God's not listening."

The raven preened its wing feathers then spoke again. "Like a mother, the universe gives the world what it needs. You are queer because people need you to be."

"Wait! Are you telling me I'm gay because of *them*?" he pointed toward the congregation, infuriated.

But the raven only voiced more kraas and continued grooming.

"How many of us have to fight this war before things change?"

The bird ignored the question and ruffled its feathers.

An awkward silence wedged them apart and Jonah changed the subject. "I didn't mean to hurt Tovy, even though he deserved it."

"Time will tell a different story," foretold the raven. Her beak tapped the bough.

The old tree rattled and cracked and crystalized into mirrored glass that had Jonah marveling at a million sublime, tinging reflections of himself. Glinting lance-shaped leaves, twigs, branches, and ribbons of coruscating bark, caught his wide-eyed amazement, until a light clicked on and switched everything transparent.

Out of breath, Tovy sets a bottle of alcohol, ointment and bandages onto his weight bench and immediately locks the door. He drops trou and carefully removes the red bandage to inspect the cut in the mirror fixed to the back of his door. Blood oozes again. He whispers, "Sonofabitch!" Fresh gauze drips with disinfectant. Tovy takes a deep breath and forces the saturated cotton against his cut. Cringes but holds it firm until the pain is gone. The bleeding eventually stops. His finger applies ointment and tape secures a clean dressing to his thigh. Tovy eases out of his clothes and forces himself to look at his likeness of Michelangelo's David. The mirror shows his self-contempt which he shatters with his fist. Tovy's perfectly muscled body separates into cracked, disjoined angles that give him brief approval and slightly bruised knuckles. He unlocks the military trunk at the foot of his bed and removes the false bottom. Pushes away books about: non-binary, third gender, sexual fluidity to retrieve garments underneath. Pink, lace-trimmed panties cover his hips and tuck away his dick. The matching frilly bra cuts into his back and fastens in the front. Tovy adjusts his pecs inside each cup then eases a simple floral dress which fits tight against his muscles, over his head and down over his body. He experiments with various poses and vogues in the mirror. Holds his cheeks and smiles.

Knock! Knock! Knock!

Tovy jumps back in fear. The knob rattles and the door shakes. "Getting dressed…" he yells through the door. Fumbles to get out of the dress and tears it taking it off. The bra comes off easy which he stashes in the trunk along with the dress. With no time to get out of his panties, he pulls up his jeans and opens the door.

His impatient father charges into his room as though he were still in the Army. "What did I tell you, young man, about locking your door?"

"Didn't realize it was…" Tovy turns his back, picks up the pair of barbells, and aggressively pumps his biceps.

"How'd things go this afternoon?" His father notices the first aid items.

"Fine, just a small cut. I'll live…"

His father observes the bloody mess is the trash can. "Any witnesses?"

"Not a soul on the lake, thanks to the storm."
"Good enough... Not a word to your mother."
Tovy's phone chimes. He quickly puts down the weights and unlocks his phone to read the message and catch his breath. He replies immediately. When his phone chimes again, he is completely gobsmacked by the incoming photo.
"Everything okay?"
Tovy coolly nods. "Yeah, a friend needs me to help him with something." He goes to put on his shirt.
But his father stops him. "What are these lines across your back?"
"You know Jael is always leavin' her mark. She can be a force sometimes." He stares his father in the face; his eyes deliberately land on the hollow space disfiguring his father's temple. "Is there anything else?" He reads the name on his father's dog tag. "Lieutenant Colonel, Linden."
Lyell backs down, lets go of his suspicions. "Well, she's a lucky girl..." He slaps Tovy's ass on his way out but stops in the doorway. "You've got school tomorrow so don't be out late." A stiffness returns to his face. "First light will be coming before your morning wood." Gives his son a stern warning. "Both will blind you." His father leaves.
Tovy shuts the door, leans his back against the broken mirror and smiles for a second. His expression changes to growing paranoia over the photo. Finishes getting dressed and turns the light off on his way out.

The mirroring Eucalyptus transformed back into evergreen form and the raven spoke again. "Tovy's life is in your hands."

"Mine??"

"Revenge is an act of passion, vengeance...an act of justice. To understand is to forgive." The bird sharpened its formidable claws against the rough bark.

"What about my life?" The words came out before Jonah could stop them. "Wait! I don't wanna know." He fluttered his lips over the gathering crowd. "Tell me, how many of us are in this fight? Because I can't count that high…"

"The world is fated by mankind's hardened sin of judgment. Greed for power, wealth and land," said the raven. "Laws are written to keep leaders in power, who exploit their religion to justify ethnic and moral persecution. Killing, conquering, enslaving…even genocide without guilt or penalty. Willingly forfeit the Earth for campaigns of war that spare few generations. These immoral weights are heaved upon humanity's scale. Time's hourglass still trickles blood."

"That doesn't answer my question," argued Jonah.

"Every soul it takes to lift the scale," the bird answered. "Humanity unravels more with every thread torn by complicities of hatred. Hatred taught with lies and fear. You must stand against all hate or be swept away by its indifference. Souls are weighed by the love they hold within. Compassion and acceptance bring change. Benevolence is learned from the chosen, from the gifted, from the extraordinary." The raven's eyes blinked at Jonah. "From you…"

"So, I'm queer and dead at seventeen? That doesn't seem fair. I've never gotten to kiss a guy, or say I love you, or seen in someone's eyes, their love for me."

"Enlightenment," said the raven, "comes from edification and science, not judgment. Finding acceptance in yourself and others, plants seeds of empathy. Empathy grows into understanding. Cultivates love and a higher purpose. Darns humanity…" The raven turned its eyes skyward. "And the scale rises…"

Jonah wrestled with his understanding of the truth. "This has to end, here at Sinner's Lake, with me!" He was beyond asking nicely, "It ends now or let the world unravel and point the way to hell."

The raven made short, continual, shrills and spoke with greater urgency. "Always live your truth, offer forgiveness, love unconditionally. But be careful of licentious temptations. They evanish love and will empty your soul before you realize. Share your story with the world and you will find—"

The arrow came out of nowhere hitting its target with a dull whisper. It happened so fast, there was nothing Jonah could do but catch the bird's eyes and nod before the acolyte laid its head over and fell.

His fingernails dug into the tree, and as he looked beyond his trembling feet at the raven on the ground, Jonah wept. A minute later he heard voices.

"Perfect shot, Tovy! You took it down, alright." His hardened face cracked a smile. Young Tovy was amped, his mouth watered, eyeballing his first distance kill. "I did what you taught me, Pa. Tried not to try when I released the bowstring."

Tovy nudged the bird with his shoe. "You gotta be hittin' when the Devil's pitching."

His father crouched down to retrieve the arrow. "God may have given us dominion over the fish in the sea, over the birds in the sky, and over every living thing that moves on the earth…" He stood up, "But sometimes son…they still find ways uh gettin' even."

Tovy shot his father a puzzled look.

Lyell shaded his eyes and looked up. "Bird dropped a right good sixty feet. The arrow point snapped when it hit." Handed his son the broken shaft with turkey feather fletching.

Tovy was about to stomp the bird when his pa grabbed his arm.

"Time to go, young man, ceremony is starting. We'll bury it later. . ."

—

22

Removed

The next thing Jonah knew he was back in his body, underwater, about to drown. Not giving up, he went for his pocket, and his fingers searched for what he hoped was still there. He grabbed onto the arrow tight until he felt the blade bite his flesh. He couldn't risk losing it. His other hand found the rope and he managed to bring the two together. Seconds later the blade cut through and Jonah was free.

He needed to get to the surface fast and swam hard against the current—pulling his body with his arms and kicking even harder. His mouth wanted air but clenched his jaw tighter. Doesn't matter, he screamed, you're a try hard, and put himself back in the race. His muscles started to seize but he refused to quit, refused to die, refused to let them win. When his mouth involuntarily opened, he pushed hard against the world and hurled his body forward. His lungs found air.

Jonah floated on his back with his heart racing. He couldn't breathe in enough air to quell the fire in his chest. Opening his eyes to heavy rain meant he was alive. What just happened? How had he made it to the surface? How did he survive? There were no justifiable reasons except one—maybe the dream wasn't entirely a dream. Too exhausted to give it more thought, Jonah welcomed rain into his thirsty mouth with laughter.

After several failed attempts, he finally had his ankle untied and tried to wiggle his toes but couldn't. Thunder peeled in the distance, and Jonah knew he had to get to shore, get out of the woods and get help. Unable to see through the curtain of rain, following the current made the most sense.

Exhausted from hard swimming, Jonah needed to rest, but with still no land in sight, he went onto his back, closed his eyes and drifted off. Weightless and eased, random images that left him in awe, came in and out of focus. His sense of safety changed when his attackers' selfie appeared. Everyone stood together in solidarity, celebrating with cool poses, hand gestures and attitude, with Jonah bobbing in the background. Seeing himself in the picture was scary enough but when their close-up faces yelled, "Trout fishing"—he woke himself, unnerved and splashed around, checking every direction again and again. Was relieved to only see passing waves. Knowing they could return brought him enough fear to keep swimming.

When the last of his adrenalin was gone, he swam on autopilot, his mind was shut down and time didn't exist. He might have been swimming in circles for all he knew and decided to rest. Afraid he might pass out for good if he floated, he tried treading water and as his legs kicked underneath him, something bumped his foot. Electrified fear sent him splashing away but then he felt it again. "Wait a minute!" Excitement overtook his panic and fighting the current, he straightened his legs and stood up, with waves lapping under his chin.

Water was at his waist when Jonah found high ground on the sandbar, hoping he might spot land, but heavy mist obscured his view beyond the rolling waves. Surrounded by water, he stood alone on the sliver of sand, tired and broken and removed. Unsure which direction to go, had to make up his mind soon, feeling the shoal washing away and water quickly rising. His body started to shiver. Jonah enfolded his arms around himself and quietly sobbed. Seconds later, he thought he heard something, wiped his eyes to see. Another splash rolled behind him. A fish leaped out of the water, and was swimming right for Jonah. He tried to rub the hallucination from his eyes as the fish swam circles around him. "Wait!" He'd seen this before and when the fish capered off in a straight line, Jonah remembered his dream, remembered what Jesus had said, and immediately dove in—in pursuit.

—

23

Miguel

By the time Jonah found land, the storm had moved on, leaving a ribbon of purple clouds against an orange and blue sunset. He crouched in the warm shallows and nervously watched a stranger in his camp up on the beach. Maybe he was one of the boys? It was already too dark to tell. Maybe a drifter or ex-con? Every time Jonah's feet tried to move, tired paranoia held him back. What if he's not alone? Jonah splashed water in his face, shook fears out of his head, and made sure the dragonfly was still on his arm before wading ashore.

He limped up the embankment with fists full of sand, ready to throw if it came to that. Stopping at a safe distance. The young man stood at a table, cooking his food and singing along with his Latin music, but when Jonah tried to get his attention, he broke into a Salsa routine.

"Hel-lo? Can you please he-lp me?"

The young man continued dancing.

Jonah swallowed hard and raised his voice. "Hello? Can you please help me?!"

Startled, the young man looked over his shoulder and saw Jonah in the sunset.

Jonah heard him yell something, saw him run toward him, squared himself and readied for a fight. There was a knife in the guy's hand, Jonah was sure of it, and the tighter his fists squeezed, the faster sand spilled to the ground. His heart raced but all of his blood pooled in his feet. The world started to spin. The sky, the lake, the beach, the approaching guy—circled around him. Jonah didn't know where to look, couldn't keep up with the spinning, his legs went numb and he dropped.

The smell of burning wood and soft music pulled Jonah from heavy sleep. He sat up quickly and tried to see, but there was only darkness beyond the crackling fire.

"Hey Papo, stay chill."

Jonah glimpsed the barefoot young man against the fire light. He carried a blanket and a cup. Jonah sighed, laid back down and closed his eyes—too exhausted to think or feel anything except relief. All he wanted was to rest beside the warmth but the constant droning of night cicadas warned otherwise.

"¡Me asustaste!" said the guy, taking a knee. "Hi!"

Jonah shook his head, not understanding.

"You scared me, bro."

"How long have I been out?" Jonah asked, quietly.

"Long enough to get you here," the guy said, pulling the blanket over Jonah. "Welcome to my Havana. Accommodations ain't much, but the night view," he paused to look up, "is cosmic and music can get loco…"

Jonah kept quiet.

"Sorry if I talk too much, Papo. Here, drink some of mama's bay leaf tea." He lifted Jonah's head. "She'd swear by it, if God would let her."

Jonah blindly took a sip and felt the spicy, hot liquid reach his stomach. "Are you out here alone?"

"Yeah, just me and the night crawlers 'til you showed up. I'm Miguel…"

Jonah enjoyed another sip but didn't share his name.

"Can I take you somewhere?"

"No…just let me rest awhile."

"Por la gracia de Dios."

His words skipped like a stone over Jonah's thoughts then disappeared.

"Want some more tea? Hungry? I can get you some—"

"Wait, what did you say?" Jonah forced open his eyes, and when the fire gave them light, saw a familiar face. It felt as though his defender had always been there, watching with invisibility, until life decided in this moment, Jonah could see him again. Miguel was more handsome than Jonah's fixed memory of him; his eyes were greener and stubble gave his juvenile face a coming-of-age roughness that blurred against Jonah's tears.

"Didn't know I was that ugly," quipped Miguel.

Entangled by his emotions, Jonah had to be sure. "Did you save a kid from drowning once?"

The question hit Miguel unexpectedly and he gave a slight nod. "Wait! You know that kid?"

Jonah pointed at himself.

"Ah, no way, bro? You're older than that Jonah kid."

"You remembered my name?"

"Hard to forget what life throws at you sometimes."

Jonah laughed through his tears.

Miguel's excitement eased. "I think I cracked your ribs that day."

"My chest hurt for weeks, made it hard to breathe, couldn't run much. Stayed home that summer. Worried the incident would get me more bullied at school. It did a lot."

"I was hoping you'd come back to the pool."

"I was too embarrassed and too afraid. Bad dreams…" remembered Jonah. "For months, I woke up gasping in a cold sweat from the same night terror, where you didn't save me. Saw myself drowned at the bottom; you know…with a hard-on. Kids would dive down, point and laugh. Sometimes they played torpedo corpse dodge with their friends. Anyway, when I finally got the nerve to ride my bike to the pool that following summer, I looked for you through the fence, but a girl was sitting in your lifeguard chair. So I left. Assumed I was the reason."

"My Papi was set up by a coworker," explained Miguel. "Bitter over his promotion, got Papi fired. That was just the start of our troubles."

"Why? What happened?"

"Mama is Cuban and Papi is Brazilian. They immigrated to the US before I was born. Rally-Whites don't want mutts taking over the town. One morning before light, police banged on our door… arrested Papi. Kept him locked up for days, but never officially charged him, just let him go. Cops still cruised our house for weeks after. I quit lifeguarding when we moved across town to be closer to family. White-folks wanted us gone, they've got their reasons, but we're still here. I'll be the first in my family to go to college. Can't wait."

As close as Miguel was, time and uncertainty kept them separated with so many questions. "Why are you out here, Miguel?"

"Don't get me wrong, I love my family and they love me back, but there's too many shoes in our house sometimes. I come out here to get away, hike around, sort things out." Miguel laughed, "I was going to ask you the same question, bro."

Silence.

"You're in rough shape."

"I just need to rest awhile."

Miguel's phone buzzed and he read the text. "Be right back…" Miguel was already up on his feet. Moments later, he sat back down to put on his shoes, "We're gonna get you outta here."

Jonah's voice rattled, "We?"

"Yeah, I'm meeting up with a friend tomorrow. His friends want to teach me to ski. I sent him a text while you were out. Said he was on his way with his dad's boat."

Jonah quickly sat up and through the firelight caught sight of the red sneaker on Miguel's foot. "Those yours?" he tried to stay calm.

"These hand-me-downs?"

Jonah gave a slight nod.

Miguel knocked sand off his other foot. "Mama used to clean this family's house. They've got money. Ex-military. I'd drop her off then pick her up later. Met their son while waiting one evening. He asked me if I wanted to get high. We started hanging out. Never at his house. Asked me to call him T. He's a wild muscle-head. We've even hooked up a few times," huffed Miguel and checked his phone.

The distant hum of a motorboat broke across the night lake.

"I have to go…" Jonah struggled to get on his feet.

Miguel rushed to help him up. "You know it's a long hike. How are you even going to see in the dark?"

"That's for me to figure out."

"T's boat will get you to the highway faster than your feet."

Jonah saw real concern on Miguel's face. "Can I ask you something? Did it mean anything to you?"

"What? Me and T fooling around? Does it have to?"

"Shouldn't it?" argued Jonah but then quickly moved on. "No, that day at the pool. You saving my life. I thought we had a connection. Something special."

Miguel stammered for an answer.

But with the boat fast approaching, Jonah was out of time. "You don't have to say anything, your hesitation already did. Thanks. . ."

Miguel grabbed his arm. "Why won't you let T help you?"

"Ask your friend," Jonah scoffed and started to walk away. "You can tell Tovy, Trout says hello."

—

24

Tovy

Crouched in the moonlit woods, Jonah watched the motorboat pull into the shallows. Tovy jumped into the surf and limp-sprinted up the beach. Jonah started to make his way down to the water, with a plan to slip onboard, and steal the boat. It was a huge risk, but he was out of options. As he crept in the swash, he heard Miguel and Tovy arguing.

"Where is he, Miguel?" yelled Tovy. "Where's that slippery fish?"

"What fish, T?" Miguel played innocent.

"Trout!! Where is he?"

Jonah pulled back to keep from being seen.

"Wrong time of year for catching trout, you know that!" Miguel pushed back.

"Don't fuck with me!" Tovy shoved Miguel out of his way, stormed his camp and then quickly returned and grabbed Miguel by his shirt. "Where is he, goddammit?"

"Just give me the boat, T."

"I'm not gonna ask you again!" Tovy pulled back his fist.

"Try looking in your closet, *Tovy*. That's your name, right?"

Jonah couldn't believe his ears.

"You don't know what you're talking about!"

"Oh yeah? You're such a fake. What would your father do, if he really knew you? Huh??"

"He'd never take your word over mine." Tovy pocked his own chest, "He's too proud of me."

"Go ahead, hit me, Tovy." Miguel stood his ground.

Tovy let his fist fly but Miguel jerked free in time.

"We're done, Tovy," said Miguel as he stepped backwards and pointed at his feet. "But thanks for the red shoes, *Dorothy!*"

Tovy tackled Miguel to the ground and threw his weight on top of him. "Those shoes kept you off the list!!" Grabbed Miguel by the throat, "I should kill you now. My friends were planning on it tomorrow anyway."

Jonah slipped up on the quiet and stood in the firelight. "Hey, Tovy?"

Tovy was almost happy to see him. "Trout, you're really alive?"

"Let Miguel go!"

"Can't do that. He knows too much!" Tovy flashed a red-face grin. "As soon as I'm done with him, we'll talk, just you and—" There was an abrupt thud and Tovy fell over.

Jonah dropped the rock onto the sand and knelt beside Miguel. Their eyes met again. It was his turn to be the hero. "Are you okay?"

Miguel nodded and looked over at Tovy. "Is he dead?"

"He lives. . ."

"¿De qué hablas?"

"Doesn't matter..." Jonah helped Miguel sit up. Strolled through his handsome, moonlit face and pulled him close. His awkward innocence was gone. Afraid he wouldn't get this chance again, Jonah asked quietly, "Can I kiss you?"

Miguel brought his lips near.

As Jonah's inexperienced lips touched Miguel's, he emerged

from the shell of his old life, left the ordinary world, vowing never to return.

—

25

List

Jonah threw lake water in Tovy's face, as he laid hogtied on the boat deck, cast in moonlight, and as he came to, Jonah took their picture.

Tovy struggled to free himself but couldn't and then realized he was stripped down to his panties.

Jonah knelt beside Tovy. "I told Miguel what you and your friends did to me. Miguel is recording this on his phone." He directed Tovy's attention to the helm. "Now six of us know the truth."

"Fuck you, *both!*"

"Who started the list, Tovy?"

"None of your goddamn business!"

Jonah showed him the selfie. "I unlocked your phone easy enough, think your friends will find our pic serious or farcical? Want me to send it?"

"Okay! Okay!" Tovy bawled. There was a long pause. "Reverend Learne started the list."

"Why would he do that??"

"You still don't get it! There's no cake for you here. Churches, schools, police, every business across town, all have the list." His voice cracked, "You're not wanted here…"

The revelation delivered a hard shock that had Jonah standing. His face turned pensive; eyes distant.

The lapping shoreline pulls at Jonah's awareness. He feels the Eucalyptus tree against his back and knows where he is—his place of finding. From this vantage, the crescent moon appears larger than normal and almost close enough to swing from. Illuminating the entire lake in neon blue and holding the audience of fiery stars and traveling clouds watchful. With no sign of Miguel, Tovy or the boat, Jonah's frustration grows and thinks he's lost his mind when the lucent moon on the water catches his eye. A wide smile hides his embarrassment for almost missing it. The view is spectacular, perfectly surreal, and lifts his spirits. A sense of urgency still has him asking—why now. What more is there to learn? A figure steps into view, black wedge platform boots stomp the sand, and a femme fatale steals the moonlight, wearing a leopard, mock-neck, one shoulder mini, with a flared ruffle sleeve and feathered cuff. Short honey blonde curls frame her made-up face. Jonah recognizes the drag queen straightaway.
"I remember you… you whispered something in my ear then disappeared. I'm guessing you know my name, so what's yours?" She struts towards him.
Jonah backs away.
"I won't bite, Jonah."
He stands there, petrified, afraid to look up at her.
She looms over him, lifts his chin, and her cat-like eyes narrow. "My name is Conscience Tripp." She head slides and her ruby lips smile. "What do you think of my dress?" She steps back and twirls. Her hand lands on her hip and bends her body into pose.
"Sorry, but I'm in a hurry."
"Wait, are you kidding me?" She throws him attitude and wags her finger. "We all have somewhere to be…" Gets in his face. "Let

me gift you some understanding. You can't change your past or those who judge you, but you can always change your attitude and the world with... haute couture!" She vogues.

"What's that?"

Conscience rolls her eyes and sighs. *"High fashion, young man."*

"Are you here to make me into a queen?"

"Honey, you're not in the running," she jokes. *"Now come with me..."* She positions him facing the moon and rests her chin on his shoulder. *"Tell me what you see."*

"A lake, the moon, some clouds, lots of stars..."

"Try harder..."

Jonah looks again and shrugs. "I don't know..."

She cups his face and smiles warmly. *"If an imperfect moon brings this much light in darkness, know that you are enough."* They take in the view together and her revelation gives Jonah some missing confidence. Feeling lightheaded, he braces himself against the tree to keep from passing out, but there is no more time for soul searching when the tree claims his arms and binds them deep into its sappy trunk where he can't pull free. Desperate for help, his frightened eyes look at Conscience.

She moves away. *"Let me gift you some understanding. Always show up for yourself because no one else will and fight like hell for what you believe in..."* She steps back. *"Love yourself so you can love others..."* Points to his crotch. *"And that isn't junk so only share it when your heart is ready. Promise me..."*

Jonah nods and she is gone again. On his own, the rippling moon holds his attention, as voices of social divisiveness and hatred and political discord ring his ears. Even Tovy's. Above all of their venom, rises her voice, and an unbending resolve comes to his face when her lost whisper finds him.

> *Sometimes love bends time and reality and expectation so that we may find the truth in ourselves. . .*

Jonah rubbed his wrists and his eyes landed on Tovy. He could play this out in so many ways. Right or not. Thought about Conscience and the raven and knew what he had to do. He worked out a plan with Miguel and then approached his tied adversary. "Tovy, you don't belong here either…" Jonah knew that forgiveness wouldn't be easy but all he could do was try. "The bird you killed in the tree that day, saved my life this afternoon." Jonah reached into his pocket and held up the small barbed shaft. "Arrows poisoned with hate, eventually find their archer, require compensation for bowman's injustice. Measure for measure. This belongs to you. . ." Jonah tossed it down onto the deck where it rattled beyond Tovy's reach. Moments later Jonah and Miguel stood in the shallows and watched the boat disappear into the night.

"How long before he finds it?" Miguel voiced his concern as he reached for Jonah's hand.

"It's a five-mile lake. Probably not before the boat runs out of fuel. He can paddle." Jonah tightened his fingers around Miguel's and pictured a determined Tovy, shifting his tied body towards the arrow that waited in the moonlight—eventually getting close enough to read the words Jonah had written on the shaft—*Free Yourself.*

—

26

Discovery

The boys found a spot by the fire and it wasn't long before Jonah was floating in his green reservoirs. "Por la gracia de Dios…" he said with a slight smile.

Miguel pulled him close and gave Jonah a kiss and then another and then offered his open mouth.

Drawing Miguel's breath into his own, Jonah allowed Miguel's tongue inside. Adrenalin and fervor made up for any pain from the beatings, but he was unprepared when Miguel rubbed his crotch. Maybe he wasn't ready. Maybe he did need saving. As he studied Miguel's beautiful face—he knew—and let his shame wash into the lake like so many baptized souls. Sand couldn't smother the fire fast enough, and in the flicker of a few lasting embers, they helped each other out of their clothes, and in the subdued light Jonah discovered that Miguel was intact. "What about HIV?"

Miguel smiled. "I'm PrEPping. Taking a drug that helps prevent exposure. Is this your first time?"

Jonah nodded slightly.

"We're good. You can touch it." Miguel guided Jonah's nervous hand.

. . .

Jonah opened his eyes against the perse dawn and waited for the few remaining stars to tell him where he was—still at Sinner's Lake—lying naked and safe under a blanket next to Miguel.

Jonah fixed on his sleeping boyfriend's breathing; watched his chest quietly rise and fall. Held his breath momentarily then exhaled along with Miguel—together.

Jonah checked his arm, his dragonfly was faded, but still there. He'd get a real tattoo soon enough.

"Hey you?" Miguel sat up and planted a kiss on Jonah's cheek. "How are you feeling?"

Jonah kissed him back then carefully pulled up the blanket to expose his foot. Swelling was down, color was back, and his toes moved a little. "Looks like I'm gonna be fine…"

"We should go soon," said Miguel.

But Jonah had other ideas and pulled Miguel on top of him and then came the blanket over them.

Miguel rested his chin on Jonah's chest, "Are you okay…with us?"

His words ricocheted out of the past, and for a second, Jonah was back at the pool—floating in the bronze glow of Miguel's wet face—watching his concerned green eyes steal light from the sun and his heart again.

"Happily, ever-after," smiled Jonah.

Miguel's eyes smiled back. "I want you inside me. . ."

Jonah was already ready, held him in his eyes, and accompanied Miguel into his unknown. Whispers and patience and spit allowed him inside, their wild coupling quickened his discovery, and lost virginity left him sweating and unfolded and in love, drifting with Miguel in boundlessness and truth.

. . .

Locking arms around their shoulders, Jonah and Miguel watched the morning sky change from blue to orange, and when the sun climbed above the lake and hit them with light—knew they were out of time.

"Hey, whatever happens, I'm not worried, because we'll always have this moment," whispered Jonah, holding tightly to Miguel. Knowing that a single arrow launched into the sky years ago, intended for one target, was always destined for their hearts. Realizing that dreams are not always just dreams. That faith is believing in something that can't be explained by science or reason. Mostly, because love is inescapable.

Looking over Miguel's shoulder, a believing smile fixed on his face—spotting the Good Shepherd standing on the sunlit hill with his feeding sheep.

Jesus smiled back at him, holding the sleeping raven cradled in his arm.

Acknowledgments

Writing a book is really hard work and more rewarding when characters from my imagination come to life and share their experiences. I couldn't have written this without the support of my husband, Greg. Your patience and understanding eased my guilt over waking up at 5 am every morning to write. I appreciated your funny moments when you quietly sat across the table and watched me type. They kept me laughing. Your encouragement brought enthusiasm for writing. Thank you to my son, Edward, for gifting me a window into the life of a Gen Z.

I am deeply grateful to my writing coach and editor, Tony Amato. Your commitment to this project and mentorship throughout this journey is invaluable. Padre, your encouragement, generous comments and sharp editing, helped me craft this powerful narrative. You have my gratitude and love always.

A very special thanks Mario Elias who edited an early draft of the manuscript.

About the Author

James E Reese spent most of his life growing up in a military home in Eastern North Carolina, where his creative energy went into writing short stories, song lyrics and poetry, until recently starting his novel writing career. In 2013, he married his partner of 11 years. They currently live in San Francisco with their teenage son. *Jonah: A Gay Teenager's Journey for Love Through the Magical Realism of Faith* is his first book.

Made in United States
North Haven, CT
06 December 2021